SAGITTARIUS SAVES LIBRA

Signs of Love #6

ANYTA SUNDAY

First published in 2022 by Anyta Sunday
4D Palm Grove, Berhampore, Wellington 6023, New Zealand

An Anyta Sunday publication
www.anytasunday.com
Copyright 2022 Anyta Sunday

ISBN 978-3-947909-48-3

Cover Design by Natasha Snow
Sagittarius and Libra Art Design by Maria Gandolfo (Renflowergrapx)

Content Edit, Line Edit & Proofread by Lynda Lamb @ Refinery
www.refineryedits.com

This book contains explicit sexual content.

Sagittarius Saves Libra

True love is on the horizon, Sagittarius. It's a good time to step out of your routine and into the unknown.

Jason Lyall wants someone to come home to, someone he can be his most ridiculous self with. Someone who loves him regardless. But no matter how hard he tries, he can never quite make that connection, and now his last girlfriend has moved on —she's engaged.

So when his identical twin begs him to swap lives for a few weeks, Jason can see the appeal. Suddenly he's living another life in a tiny Australian town, contending with weird, wild, and wonderful things the likes of which he's never encountered before. Like spiders. Like snakes.

Like his new neighbour, Sergeant Owen Stirling, who is all kinds of . . . *suspicious*.

Prepare to be caught in a merry mix-up, Libra. It's a dance of side-stepping and seduction.

Set in a made up town in Tasmania. A few artistic liberties have been taken.

Thank you to Becky Coates for providing critical Tasmanian details.

This book uses New Zealand grammar and punctuation.

 Earnest Point Police
@earnestpointcops

3 days, people. C'mon. You know who you are.

 Earnest Point Police
@earnestpointcops

A whole month without a traffic violation. Can we do it? YES WE CAN

Chapter One

Wind flapped Jason Lyall's open coat toward the window of his favourite restaurant, where Caroline sat over candlelight, laughing. With her current boyfriend.

Half a year ago, Jason had tried to make her laugh like that. He'd always missed the mark—no matter how much he wished for it, they'd never clicked. Not like *that* . . .

He smiled wistfully. Not for Caroline, but for the idea of her. A partner to come home to each night. Someone to be his most ridiculous self with. Someone who loved him regardless.

Because of, even.

He schlepped past the restaurant, bowing his head over a text message to his brother (*be there in 2 mins*), and traipsed through the dark up the light-speckled hill toward the villa he'd grown up in. The quarter-acre patch his parents had left him.

The wind tossed dark hair into his eyes; he concentrated on the tickle over his skin and not the hollowness expanding on the inside. When exactly did he get this pathetic?

He chuckled.

Silly.

He used to be vibrant. Full of energy. All colour on a grey day.

Now, at twenty-six, five years after finishing university, he was . . . bored? Boring? Lonely? Antsy?

Not that he could really complain. He was an accomplished pianist, he'd travelled the world, performed with international orchestras, he had his own home. It was just . . .

He pushed the vision of happy Caroline out of his mind, laughing at himself. *Pull it together.*

He waved to his brother from the gate and closed it behind him. Tall lavender either side of the path bent with another gust. Carl pushed off the porch chair and rose to his feet.

Jason's breath caught.

It always did, seeing his brother. It wasn't any one particular feature that momentarily shook Jason; it was the combination. Carl was medium height, his smile dimpled either side of his cheeks, his bright blue eyes thickly framed with black lashes. A slightly upturned nose gave him a cute air, and there was a tiny freckle at his jaw.

It was Jason's face. His exact face.

He'd be used to it if they'd grown up in the same family, but Jason and Carl had met accidentally three years ago, when Jason had performed Bach and Chopin in Sydney. One of those Holy Shit moments that rarely happen in life, and he'd never thought would happen to *him*.

Carl was his twin.

After the initial shock, they'd swapped stories, speculated, and hired a private detective to probe into the matter. They learned they'd been born to a teenage mum whose aunt had adopted one of them. The other—Jason—had been put up for adoption.

Since then, they'd loosely kept in touch, but other than genetics he and Carl had little in common—not even a birthday, since Jason was born on December 21st and Carl on the

22nd, fifteen minutes later. Carl showing up short notice like this . . . it was a bit mind-boggling.

It seemed more the sort of out-of-left-field type of thing a Sagittarian would do.

In fact, this visit reminded Jason of the Jason he used to be.

The Jason he wanted to be again.

Before another ache could take him hostage, he smiled and opened his arms for an awkward embrace. Carl laughed, and the rhythm of it—just like his own—set off another wave of goosebumps.

Jason withdrew and let them inside. Carl peeked around the villa's airy rooms with their sparse, elegant furnishings, while Jason uncorked a much needed bottle of wine. His eyes flickered between bottle and brother.

There were a few differences between him and Carl, of course. Carl kept his hair shorter and had developed more bicep, judging by the fit of his shirt. And their styles were at opposite ends of the spectrum. Carl's was casual: baggy jeans, T-shirt, an open flannel shirt over that. Sturdy workman's boots. Jason preferred tight jeans, cashmere pullovers, colourful scarves. Ankle boots. Suits, when he was performing.

Carl hummed and finally strolled to the kitchen island. He took up one of the wineglasses like it was a pint and chugged half of it down.

Jason raised a brow. "To what do I owe the pleasure?"

Carl said "I had to get outta Earnest Point" in his mildly Australian accent.

Okay . . .

"Earnest Point" was Carl's small hometown in Tasmania, but there were hundreds of places he could have escaped to. Flying two connections to *Wellington* . . .

Jason stared, waiting.

Carl tossed back the second half of his drink. "My ex is

spontaneously getting married in three weeks. He wants me at the wedding."

He. Carl had mentioned a boyfriend before; every time, a little shot of *something* curled around Jason's belly.

Carl's brow furrowed as he stared at his empty glass. Jason sensed pain under the intense glare and poured him more wine. "Sounds like an uncomfortable situation?"

"Small community, y'know? Everyone knows everyone. Pete and I ended things pretty neat. And Nick's a good bloke. I've been keeping it together in front of them, so if I suddenly said no, it wouldn't look good."

"Could you make something up? Work related, maybe?"

"Well, I sorta said I'd be the best man, didn't I?"

Jason groaned. "What . . . *why?*"

"Put on the spot, y'know? Slipped out."

There was something beseeching in Carl's expression that had Jason's pulse ticking wildly.

He pinched the stem of his wineglass.

No way.

Surely *that* wasn't why Carl had come here.

Carl cleared his throat. "So I was thinking—"

"You can't be serious!"

"I didn't finish."

"I can read your mind."

Carl's eyes sparkled with momentary humour. "Twin thing?"

"Hardly." Jason gestured wildly with his finger. "It's all over your face. You want me to go to this wedding in your stead."

"Not quite." Carl flashed those deep dimples, and Jason suddenly knew what it felt like to be on the end of his own foolery. "More . . . swap lives. For three weeks."

∼

AT THE BOTTOM OF THE BOTTLE, MUCH HEAD-SHAKING LATER, Jason once more exclaimed, "You're out of your mind."

"Am I? I'm thinking this the most ingenious idea I've ever had."

Jason paused and stared at Carl over the kitchen island. "That doesn't bode well for you." He opened another bottle— unusual for him, since his tolerance was only so-so and he preferred his head clear. But . . . this . . . All the details Carl had already planned out . . .

It was ridiculous.

And yet . . .

That niggling curiosity about his 'other family'. He wondered who they were, what they were like, whether they would like him . . .

He sploshed more wine into their glasses. "Isn't this the kind of situation where you're meant to find a fake boyfriend and make everyone think you're managing fine?"

Carl pounded out a horrified laugh. "In Earnest Point?"

"Oh, but you'd fly four hours over here to ask your twin to pose as you in your nosey little town for three weeks."

At least Carl had the grace to grimace. "Look, I can't be there at all. Every sight of him is a punch. He needs me helping with stuff every other day, and I can't tell him to back off. We all live in the same curtain-twitching little community. It'd be easier if 'I'—*you*—were there acting super cool with everything on my behalf."

"How would I even pass for you? Surely your family would figure it out? My accent's a bit off for starters. Hell, I don't know enough about animals to run a pet shop, and I can't stop playing for three weeks! I have to be ready to join rehearsals for a concerto in June. Erwin Schuloff."

"It's a corner shop—like a bigger dairy. A *convenience store*, with a couple of aisles for pet stuff." Carl straightened on his stool. "I could spend the weekend prepping you—a few tweaks here and there and not a soul would know. I have a piano at my house, you can play that. They're pretty much all the same, right?"

All the same? Jason stared at him for a moment, incredulous, then shook it off. "Doesn't Pete know about me? Surely he'd notice I'm not the real Carl?"

"He won't. You know no one knows I know about you."

Jason got whiplash following all those knows.

But he did . . . know. The first time they'd talked about this, Carl had said it didn't feel right to let his 'mum' know he'd found out—she'd never brought up adopting him, let alone ever mentioned a secret brother. Carl figured it was important to her that he accepted his family as it was. So he kept mum, so to speak.

Jason got that. Carl had been brought up by his aunt posing as his mum, while his birth mother lived close by; there must've been a good reason for that—if it did come out . . .

Some secrets were best kept buried.

"You've seriously told no one else?"

"Only you."

It'd been different for Jason. His mum and dad *had* told him he was adopted. They'd always said if he wanted to know more, he could ask, but until he'd run into Carl, he hadn't felt compelled to. And by that time, they'd already died.

Half his blood relatives lived just over the Tasman Sea.

He'd always told himself it didn't really matter. His real family was his own mum and dad, the family he'd grown up with. He didn't miss anyone else in his life.

But . . .

He glanced around the pristine villa, his childhood home. So big; so empty his footsteps echoed.

He shouldn't be considering this.

Okay, so he had the time, sort of—he was between engagements right now, but he still had a life here.

Carl poked around his living room, like he was acquainting himself with that life. Studying it. He moved to the grand piano, stopped at the keys, tinkered and plucked up a magazine Jason had perched on the stand in front of the notes to Schulhoff's piano concerto no.1. Honestly, beyond that piano and this house, what life *did* he have here, really?

Carl smirked and flipped through the pages, then brought the magazine over, slapped it on the kitchen counter and spun it around. He tapped a biro-circled paragraph. "Twin thing? I'm addicted to this shit too."

Jason reread this week's horoscope. He didn't *need* to read it to know what it said, but he needed the moment to process the shiver shooting through him.

Be bold. Take chances, Sagittarius! Loneliness might be following you around recently, but true, heart-warming company is waiting on the horizon. A good time to step out of the daily routine and into the unknown. Escape into nature. It's bound to refresh your soul.

He swallowed. He couldn't do this because of a few measly words on glossy paper.

He didn't even truly believe in this stuff. It just sometimes . . . made him laugh.

Or hit a nerve.

He pulled out his phone. One after the other, all the weekly horoscopes that came up in his search said variations on the same thing. It was time to do what Sagittarians did best: head out for an adventure.

He bit his lip. "Are you sure your family wouldn't notice?"

"Eh. If you're acting a bit off they'd assume it's to do with Pete and the wedding. Or, y'know, you could tell them you've come down with something."

"And if they found out?"

"The only way they could is if you tell them. So just don't do that."

Jason's phone vibrated in his hand. Instagram notification. Automatically, he checked it out—and froze.

Caroline, her boyfriend, champagne, Caroline's hand splayed across her chest showing off a bejewelled finger.

Engaged!

His heart flipped and dropped to his feet. He tossed his phone to the side and looked Carl in the eye.

"This piano of yours. What sort of state is it in?"

Earnest Point Police
@earnestpointcops

If you're gonna commit a crime (no rec), be sure you're not afraid of the dark, and, in the case of our holding cell, arachnophobic.

Chapter Two

J ason hadn't crammed this hard since his last university
exam.

He studied a map of Earnest Point and a file of
pictures, memorised names and Most Important Details: the
layout of relevant houses; how to work the convenience-slash-
pet store; places Carl liked to go; where he bought his coffee;
what days he ate out; when he headed to the local pub; how he
and his 'cousin'—cough—*mother*, Cora, dissected their weekly
horoscopes (they read out one another's). Also, how strange
that obsession ran in the family?

Carl quizzed him on the fly while they donned each other's
clothes.

The heavy boots felt odd around his feet, the jeans weirdly
airy. The T-shirts he could live with, but the oversize flannel
over top made him want to cry. It just . . . hung there. He
frowned at himself in the full-length mirror. Flannel did
nothing for him.

"Mum's birthdate?" Carl asked from his perch at the end
of Jason's bed.

"July twenty-fourth. Leo."

"Allergies?"

"Pollen, pineapple, and bitchy behaviour."

"Cora's high-five flick."

Jason turned and slapped Carl's raised hand, following up with a beat pressed together, drumming their fingertips. "What's this one about?"

Carl shrugged. "Something we've done since I was a kid. Her way of bonding, I guess . . ."

They went quiet. It must have been strange, learning she was his birth mother. Everything she did would now be filtered through that new lens.

Jason prodded the cheat sheet on the dresser. He'd memorised the layout of the town, the street names, all the important people in Carl's circles—and who he might meet out and about. But there was one name they hadn't spoken much of yet. "Okay. Owen Stirling?"

"Sergeant Stirling, one of three cops in town. He lives next door. We don't get on; I stay out of his way, and he mostly stays out of mine."

"Mostly?"

"He might have clocked me for a few tickets?"

"Ah. That's why you don't like him."

"And sometimes he looks at me like he's checking me against a register of wanted criminals."

"Are you? On a register of wanted criminals?"

Carl grinned. "Anyway, you probably won't run into him much—" Carl's phone shrilled. He took one look at the screen and grimaced. "Speak of the devil . . ."

"What was that about not running into him much?"

Carl laughed nervously and thrust the phone into Jason's hand. "You answer."

"Me? What? Why? You're right here!"

"Soon you'll be me around a whole town. Baby steps."

Carl did him a real solid and prodded the accept button.

Jason glared at him.

"Hello? Is that Carl?" The voice on the other end was resonant and warm, spoken from deep down in the chest, a captivating rumble.

A strange ticklish panic shot through Jason and he nodded. *Then* used actual words. "You betcha, mate."

Carl's jaw dropped open and mouthed *what the hell?*

Jason smacked his forehead. He'd been going for an Australian accent?

Sergeant Owen Stirling also seemed to have paused. "Carl Birch?"

Jason toned it down. "Yep."

The line crackled. What did that mean? How much sweat was normal for this kind of show? He fanned his flannel.

"Great. I was wondering if you're available to come down to the station for a quick chat?"

Jason mouthed to Carl, *Unpaid tickets?*

A shrug. *Probably?*

He blew the bangs out of his eyes.

Immediately, Carl made a note on their To Do list. *Haircut.*

Jason yelped out "No!"

The sergeant's deep voice rumbled down the line again. "Excuse me?"

Oops. He'd gone and—quite emphatically—denied a cop. Would that get him in some kind of trouble? He rushed on. "I mean, I sure would *love* to meet you, Sergeant Owen, ahh, Stirling. *Sir.*"

Um . . . did that sound . . . kind of raspy? Kind of breathless? Kind of like he was begging, in the vicinity of a bed with satin sheets?

One look at Carl's horrified gape confirmed it.

After another pause, the sergeant spoke again. "This connection is . . . shocking. Anyway, better we speak in person. When are you available?"

Well not now! His flight didn't go out until later this morning. "Can't it wait?"

Why-why-why did all his intonations land wrong? Nerves were making him sound like he got paid by the minute.

He cleared his throat and tried again. "Or should I come tonight?"

"No-no, tomorrow will be fine."

"Whenever you want."

Carl dropped his pen. Jason winced.

Sergeant-Owen-Stirling-Sir made a small sound that might have been a snort, cleared his throat and signed off.

Jason went right ahead and flopped face first into his pillows. "Oh my God."

Carl echoed him. "Oh my *God*."

Laughing, Jason rolled over. "Are you sure about this?"

Carl rubbed his forehead with two fingers and nodded. "We'll practice some vocab. You'll be fine once you settle in. For the first couple days, say you've been a bit feverish. I get croaky like that when a cold comes on."

"Give me your credit card. If I'm paying your fines . . ."

Carl hesitated, then fished it out. "Fine. It has a limit, don't go crazy."

"On what? There are three stores."

They exchanged phones—logging out of anything vitally private—each adding a few numbers to the directory in case. This was the hardest part for Jason; he was loathe to part from his baby, but the break from social media . . . it would be good for him.

The only thing they didn't swap was their passports. Jason might be willing to pretend around his brother's little town for the summer, but he wasn't about to break any international laws.

"So, are we good to go?" Jason asked.

Carl grinned and checked the To Do list. "One last thing."

~

EXHAUSTION MIXED WITH EXHILARATION AS JASON FINALLY dragged himself up the dark driveway to his brother's house. He keyed open a squealing door, stepped inside, and screamed.

Shit!

Someone was there. In the dark. At the end of the hallway.

He shoved Carl's wheelie suitcase toward the intruder. It smacked into the man in black and—

Glass shattered.

He clasped a hand over his heart and laughed.

A full-length mirror. God*dammit*, he'd almost had a heart attack. It was the new haircut. He hadn't recognised himself with hair cropped short—and all that flappy flannel.

He found the blessed light switch, cringed at the mess of glass, and palmed his knees. "Fine start, Jason. Excellent."

A pounding knock came from behind him and he leapt again. What on Earth? Eleven at night? Not exactly visiting hours.

Another knock. The voice that followed was even deeper than it'd been on the phone earlier, but still had a certain unmistakable *je ne sais quoi*. Sergeant Owen Stirling Sir. "Carl? You all right in there?"

Great, here for two minutes and he'd already attracted law enforcement.

His nerves pounded; he was a quiet litany of fucks as he straightened his flannel and matted down that one stubborn bit of hair that wanted to pop up like he was a fluffy duckling. "Just a sec!"

He used that time to haul in a deep breath, then slapped on a grin and pulled open the door. He could do this. Smile and nod, keep it casual—

Yikes!

Whatever he'd expected to find on the other side of the

door, *this* wasn't it. Carl had pictures of most folks that Jason might run into, but only one of the sergeant and that was from a distance, no more than a tallish figure in the shade of a beech tree. He'd imagined him older—much older. Mid-fifties, maybe, with tired eyes and a kindly smile. What he definitely *hadn't* imagined was late twenties, dark eyes, a firm grimace, and . . . out of uniform.

Like *really* out of uniform.

An entire naked chest rose and fell before him, slightly exaggerated no doubt from the mad dash he'd done over here. Thick with hair, which was something Jason had never managed. And matted with sweat. All that skin tapering to his waist *shimmered.*

"Carl?"

A pair of long legs packed into bulging green boxer shorts was attached to the bare torso, and further down, past corded thighs, large toes peeked out of jandals—ah, *thongs.* Thongs.

Jason's gaze travelled on instinct back up to that stomach. *Ribboned* with muscle. Actual, defined musculature. He'd never seen anything like it in real life before. He checked the admittedly ridiculous (and almost irresistible) impulse to reach out and feel those contours. Not that his eyes were deceiving him!

This was like . . . looking at the man Jason wished he were. So gloriously put together.

A hot bundle of envy settled low in his stomach. Jesus, he was tired.

"*Carl?*"

Jason snapped his head up, up, up to the sergeant's concerned expression.

"I heard screaming. You all right?"

Jason swiped a hand through his hair. "It was, ah . . ." On the heels of a long day of airports, planes, and a winding taxi ride, his brain was past its best, but not so far past that he lost his self-respect. "Ah . . . kangaroo."

The sergeant looked over his shoulder at the glass mess down the hall. "A kangaroo?"

"Yeah. Big one. Tried to take me out."

The sergeant passed one of those large hands over his mouth and rubbed. The light caught his eyes, making them shine as brightly as his blond hair. "Looks like you made a lucky escape."

"Oh, yeah. It bounced right out the, ah, back door."

"Of course."

Jason leaned against the doorframe and suppressed a yawn. "Got to *love* back doors."

A raised brow.

"Makes life interesting." He smiled with adventurous spirit. A glimmer of the old Jason making a return. "Never know what'll come in next."

The sergeant blinked slowly and glanced away. That hand was back, scrubbing his jaw. "Well. You seem to have survived. I should . . ." He hitched a thumb toward the dividing fence.

Jason got it. "Bedtime, yeah. Thank you for checking in. Just in case, you know, I needed help with my backdoor."

A startled peal of laughter and the shake of a golden head. "Night, then."

"Night, Sergeant Stirling. Sir."

"Owen is fine. I'm off the clock."

Off the clock or not, it really wasn't hard, imagining him in uniform. First impressions said he was the protective type. The kind who could be hard-arsed when he needed to be, and also good-humoured when the occasion called for it. Not to mention half naked when required. Something in his smile suggested he was perfectly proportioned in *all* aspects of life.

In fact, he was remarkably like Caroline's boy—*fiancé*. The kind of guy women preferred. The kind of guy who never ended up alone in their house playing Mozart to disguise a lack of company.

Probably he had a wife. A wife who was eagerly awaiting his return, proud of her husband's heroic jump into action at the sound of Jason screaming bloody murder.

He gazed at Owen and let out a longing, envious sigh. "Guess I'll be seeing more of you soon."

Owen paused, one foot on the stairs behind him, moonlight swathed over all that goosebump-pebbled skin. Then, with a short nod, he strode back across the boundary—to his wife, two dogs, and child on the way—and Jason slouched into his new (empty) house.

It was cool inside, clean-ish. As Carl had promised, an old upright piano sat nestled against the wall in the lounge, covered in stacks of paper. It wasn't his grand, but it would do well enough.

He cleared the paper and the dust off it and sat on the cushioned stool, hoping it wasn't too out of tune. Stopped before pressing the ivory.

Instead of hiding in music, he should be embracing the chance . . . to have family again. To make a million memories before the summer was over.

To come away with all the answers of his heart.

His fingers flew over the keys.

Earnest Point Police
@earnestpointcops

Forecast says wet and windy today. Please don't do anything stupid. We don't want to have to trudge out in that.

Chapter Three

The top of the piano sat open, as he'd left it last night, his tuning kit spread out on the stool. It was a trusty old beast, the likes of the one he'd had in high school, but it hadn't been played in a long time; some tender loving care was definitely required. A mission to complete later.

First on the agenda this morning, after a breakfast of cornflakes, was to shower: check. Dress in god-awful flannel: check. Grab the keys and drive to the station before it was time to open the shop.

With a nervous hop in his step, he headed outside. The garage door rumbled open and he sidled past shelves of tools and assorted stuff toward Carl's Jeep. A Jeep that was not only unlocked, but also had its back window fully open. Carl clearly trusted this ol' town. He'd better remind Carl not to be quite so carefree with his own ride.

He settled himself into the driver's seat, inserted the key, and did a double take toward the passenger seat.

In a jiffy, five-seconds tops, he was out of the car, out of the garage and jumping up and down shuddering all over. Holy shit. He'd seen spiders before, but none—repeat *none*—in his life had been the size of his hand. Bigger. The size of . . . of Owen's hand. Splayed.

He pressed the buzzer, shutting the garage door, and shivered again. "Right. You can have the car."

Wind tunnelled through dark-leafed trees, and heavy clouds rumbled in from the horizon. Somewhere in the distance, a dog barked. Nice enough morning to walk. It was only, like, two kilometres. No sweat.

Nope, no sweat at all. Though, it was hard to tell with the sudden rain that pounded over him. It soaked through all his clothes, the wet material chafing his thighs as his shoes squelched with every step along a bush rimmed, pavement-less road.

Still. Definitely beat Uber-ing a huntsman.

Headlights flashed in his peripheral vision and Jason momentarily stumbled in the gutter. He grinned toward the vague outline of Owen beckoning with his fingers—difficult to see, what with the rain—as an ordinary-looking navy car pulled up alongside him. He thanked his lucky stars and opened the passenger door. He wasn't exactly in the best shape to sit in a dry car, but . . .

One jump, and he was inside.

Owen shook his head in mystified amusement, snatching his perfectly pressed, lint-free blazer out from under Jason's descending backside just in time and laying it across the back seat. He looked every bit as Jason expected he would in uniform. Smart, professional, a little bit intimidating. Very respectable, everything in place. A dark tie the colour of the blazer lay neatly over a navy shirt with matching epaulettes, embroidered with three gold chevrons. The crest on the arm read Tasmania Police. It added to his . . . air. An air of calm authority. He'd shaved too, the scent of his aftershave mingling with all the rain Jason had brought in.

Jason caught a flash of dark eyes on him and shuffled himself forward in the seat. "Drenched. Sorry about that."

Owen raised an eyebrow and returned those deep orbs to the road. "Whoever would have imagined *Carl* hoofing it to town?"

Shit. He was raising suspicions already. He'd better channel his inner . . . farm. No way the *real* Carl would freak out over eight hairy legs. "There's a, ah, little problem with the Jeep."

"And your first thought is to walk in a storm rather than call a mate for a ride? Or ask your neighbour?" Owen glanced pointedly at him.

Jason laughed nervously and patted Owen's shoulder. "Have I said thanks for pulling over?"

"It would be a first."

Right. Speeding tickets. "To be fair, the other times you pulled over, you were in a patrol car, and I wasn't exactly at the other end of your generosity."

Owen huffed a laugh and made a left into town. The main street. If he recalled the layout correctly, the station would be tucked away on the next left at the roundabout.

The car paused at a pedestrian crossing to let a woman in a red trench coat, hood up, walk across. Despite the rain, she twisted and gave Owen a friendly wave, and then smiled brightly.

Jason's heart rammed in his chest and he clutched at his seat. Her dark hair, her sharp nose, the shape of her eyebrows . . .

The veil of rain could not mask the resemblance.

Cousin Cora.

His birth mother.

~

OWEN PULLED UP OUTSIDE THE STATION, JOLTING TO A STOP THAT had Jason's belt tightening across his chest. It certainly snapped him out of wherever seeing his mother for the first time had sent him. Strange, excited, hiccupy feelings. God, his palms were sweating. He was due to meet her around ten tomorrow morning, according to Carl. What would he say? What did he want to know?

How could he find out without giving himself away?

Jason looked over to the driver's side. Owen was sitting back in his seat, studying him carefully.

A shiver scuttled through him at the intense scrutiny. He stopped wiping his palms on his thighs and laughed nervously as he fiddled with the belt. "Let's pay those fines."

Two eyebrows rose. "Fines?"

A discomforting jump in his belly. "Isn't that what you wanted to see me about?"

"No."

"Okay . . . then, what?"

Owen opened his door. "Come on inside."

Jason's heart ricocheted against his rib cage as he splashed after Owen into the old sixties concrete block that housed all the legal authority in Earnest Point. At a wave from Owen, the woman behind the reception desk buzzed open a door; Jason followed hesitantly through into a workroom dominated by four large desks, two occupied—an older man who nodded tightly at them as they passed then continued his phone call, and a woman around Owen's age, currently at leisure in front of a frozen computer screen.

"Hey, Jane."

Jane cracked a smile at Owen. "What's the status on IT support?"

"The storms blocked Silvia's road—she says she won't make it today." Owen grinned and tapped the desk beside Jane's mug. "But the coffee machine's still working."

She chuffed and returned her attention to a well-worn copy of *Crossword Puzzle Omnibus*.

Owen peered over the edge. "Still stuck on five down?

"What's with this? It's impossible."

"They're never impossible when you know the words."

"Impossible. By the way, we had a storm streaker this morning. Tweeted about it."

Owen checked his phone. "6 a.m.—Exposure. Duck pond. Gentleman in the nude claiming to be able to make it storm. #investigating."

A loud bark came from behind them and a wet golden lab raced forward, towing a harried young man—twenty tops—after it. "Mary!"

Owen laughed and dropped to his knees, meeting a series of excited licks. Mary wagged her tail, then caught Jason's quiet step backwards and started to bark again. Jason backed up to the desk, pulse jumping, and half leapt onto it, arse knocking something over as he tried.

"Mary, quit it. It's just Carl. You know Carl, he's in here every other week."

Jason grimaced and tried laughing off his reflexive panic. "I stink of storm. Probably smell like a power cut about to happen." He shot a grin at Owen. "You'd better get your coffee, quick."

Mary's barking continued.

"She's never like this." Owen frowned and cocked his head at Jason again. "Except with suspects."

Suspects?

"She's triggered by suspicious behaviour. Lies."

Jason gulped.

The shyly smiling man Mary had dragged in took hold of her and clipped on the leash. "Sorry, Uncle Owen."

Owen patted Mary's head and took his inquisitive gaze off

Jason for a moment. He clapped a hand on his nephew's shoulder. "You're all right, Alex. Thanks for dog-sitting."

"Yep, um, I also had an accident with the food you bought? I put it on the roof of my car while I was settling her in and . . . there's dog food all over the highway. I'll replace it, promise."

Owen scruffed up his nephew's hair, more amused than annoyed.

"Rightio, come on you lot." Jane rapped on the desk. "Starts with an A. 'Slowly'."

Before Owen could fix his dark, shiver-inducing look on him again, Jason leaned back towards Jane. "Can I see?"

Jane blinked. "You into crosswords now, Carl? Or are you procrastinating? You must be in big trouble this time." She handed him the book as Alex turned toward the exit, sans Mary. "Have a stab at it, but I'm not gonna butter him up for you. Again. Capiche?"

Jason jerked his gaze away and plucked up a pen. Big trouble?

What hadn't Carl told him?

Owen was a hot prickle at his back, watching him fill in the little crossword boxes. A-D-A-G-I-O. "And then three across—"

"D-O-G-G-E-D!" She cheered. "Oi, Owen. Be nice to him this time, you know how long I've been stuck on that."

Those prickles shifted, at his side now, like Owen was capturing a mug shot of his profile.

Heat lanced up Jason's throat. He wasn't sure he was made for whatever kind of interrogation this would be.

He shoved a hand through his hair and met folded arms and dark eyes. "Let's get this over with. Where do you want me?"

Owen's eyes flashed, eliciting a short sharp shiver that Jason couldn't quite categorise.

Owen took a quick step back. "Over"—he pointed across the room—"the back chair."

"Over the back chair," Jason repeated, nodding.

Jane spat out a mouthful of coffee.

Owen shut his eyes and rubbed that jaw of his. It was already starting to sprout stubble.

"Over at the back chair," Jason tried again with a small grin for the slip up. He had so much on his mind, nerves tangled for the day to come . . . he just wasn't thinking straight.

Mary gave another bark, and Jason quite happily leaped to his feet and marched for said chair. It sat in a corner along with another, a sad looking pot plant, and a narrow door open onto a supply closet, all cordoned off by shoulder-height screens.

He sank into the smaller chair of the two, trying for nonchalance. The back was too short for it to be graceful though, and getting low enough to lounge the top half of his torso put his still rather damp crotch on full display at the chair's edge. Nope, he needed to sit up again—

Mary barked and he froze in place.

Owen planted himself in the chair opposite, looked up from his official-looking clipboard, and dropped it. He scooped it off his feet, murmuring "Of course."

Mary whined and nuzzled between Owen's sturdily parted legs, and Owen petted her, grimacing. "I know, I know."

Meanwhile, Jason managed to reseat himself and his dignity. He smiled widely. *Nothing strange here at all. Just regular ol' drowning in flannel Carl.*

Owen eyed his lips, and Jason stretched them wider.

"Do you need a minute for the bathroom?"

Quickly, Jason dropped the smile. "You wanted to chat about something I've done?"

A pause. "Is there anything you think I should know about?"

Jesus Carl, what have you got yourself into? "Not that I can think of?"

A massively arched brow. "Is that right?"

"Yep."

Mary barked.

"I mean, no?"

"Go on."

"I didn't run someone over, did I? During any of my speeding antics?"

Owen set the clipboard on a freestanding shelf, leaned forward with his elbows on his thighs, and clasped his fingers together. "My original reason for this chat had nothing to do with questionable driving skills."

Original reason? There was a new one? Jason picked invisible lint from his soggy flannel. "What, ah, would that chat have been in reference to?"

A snort. But any traces of it vanished when Jason lifted his eyes. Instead, Owen was rubbing his brow like he'd been bestowed with a rather grand headache. "It would have been *in reference to* Pete and Nick's upcoming nuptials."

Oh.

The big day. The whole reason he was here. Conning a cop.

Oh God, he was going to end up in cuffs, wasn't he?

Jason rubbed pearls of sweat off his nape. "What about the nuptials?"

"Never mind that now. We have more important things to discuss." Owen looked him squarely in the eyes, and Jason was shot through with a guilty shiver. It swished around in his chest and dove lower, and it was making him tap his foot like he had as a kid when he first started school, or before a big exam. If this continued too long, he'd start breathing funny.

"More important things. Right. Right. Like—" Jason searched around him for something innocuous to suggest, but a dark supply cupboard full of photocopying paper and a limp plant weren't much inspiration. "Um, how my convenience store could be more convenient? Deal on donuts maybe? I'm sure I can make that magic happen."

Owen leaned in, all that weight crafting a rich wall of heat that definitely made Jason breathe funny. "Something's different about you."

"I've been a bit feverish!"

"Hm?"

"Gets me croaky . . . I end up doing things I normally wouldn't."

"Like hiking in the rain?"

Um . . . "Yep."

The quiet laughter that followed sounded more like a warning than a suggestion of humour. "Let's try again."

Shit, shit, shit.

He'd been made. And day one had barely started. His breathing came out shallow and quick; his heart was not made for all this dark-eyed intensity.

He looked away.

Looked back.

Looked away again.

That . . . intensity shifted and Owen's voice rumbled, lower, "Is there—" just enough pause for Jason to lose his breath completely "—anything I should know about?"

"I'm not a criminal! Promise!" He came off his chair in his impassioned declaration, damp thighs jolting toward Owen, still curved in his seat. Somehow Jason halted an inch before smacking his crotch in the cop's face. Jesus. He was . . . he was not having the most graceful day. In his peripheral vision, Owen's colleagues turned their heads in interest.

Owen rose to his feet, raising a brow, his lips . . . quirking? "A name would be nice."

"Oh." He lowered his voice, almost to a whisper. "Um . . . here's the thing though . . ."

A long look.

"Is there a way that no one finds out about this? Because it's a very sensitive issue. I haven't ditched Carl in a shallow grave and assumed his life or anything, this is mutually agreed. And I used my own passport to get here . . ."

Something akin to *a-ha!* sparkled in Owen's eyes.

Jason glanced toward their audience. Too close for comfort. If he was going to spill, he had to make very sure the truth didn't flood the whole town. "Is there an interrogation room you can take me to?"

"Not currently."

"What about the holding area?"

"You want to tell me behind bars?"

"Anywhere we have—" Jason glanced around them, whispering, "privacy."

"This is as private as it gets."

Jason gnawed his lip, eyed the supply closet and grabbed a handful of Owen's blazer. The aim was to haul him into it, but wow. None of that muscle budged.

Slowly, Owen looked down to where Jason had curled his fist, scrunching fabric. "Grabbing an officer is an offense, hmm?"

Jason raised both his hands in horrified surrender. In his panic, his voice got . . . breathless. "Manhandle me then. Shove me into the closet. I'll give you what you want."

Owen opened his mouth and clapped it shut again. "God help me," he murmured. "Mary, stay." And he gestured Jason to follow.

The closet was . . . not made for two. Certainly not when one of those two was Sergeant Owen Stirling Sir. Owen folded himself inside, ducking his head from the low inner ceiling, and Jason crammed himself into the remaining wedge of space.

Shelves crowded in on three sides, and a few edges pressed at Jason's lower back and under his arse.

Barely an inch separated them—in fact those folded arms bumped Jason's chest—and that rich wall of heat from before upgraded to volcanic levels. Aftershave quickly overwhelmed the scent of paper and dust.

Jason breathed in deeply. Bergamot and . . . lavender?

Definitely some lavender in there. Much nicer than his own —and he *liked* his own. He should find out what it was—

But maybe not now.

At the semi-exasperated look on Owen's face, Jason stopped breathing so obviously through his nose and grinned.

"Um. Right." Jason reached for the door and jerked it shut.

It was much darker without the light of the room pouring in. The little lightbulb over their heads cast a warm glow over the shelves, but with Owen's head bent forward their faces were shadowed. A strange thrill zapped through Jason, like the time he'd broken curfew to climb the school roof. Naughty. Exhilarating. Secrecy did that.

The rhythm of their quietly huffing breaths was broken by Owen. "Who are you really?"

Jason winced. "Carl's twin."

"That much I figured out, sweetheart."

"Ha. Right. I'm Jason. Jason Lyall. Please don't throw me in jail?"

Arms unfolded and a warm palm squeezed his shoulder. "Calm. Impersonation isn't actually an offence. Unless you're impersonating an officer, and Carl is no officer."

"You're right about that!" In fact, very shortly, he'd be having a few words with his brother.

Fingers shifted over his damp shoulder and dropped away, and Jason shivered.

Secrecy was . . . a lot to handle.

Time to get out of here before he sweated himself into a puddle. Why wouldn't this bit of wood move?

"I have more questions," Owen stated.

Was his name not enough? Jason fiddled with the door. "Is there a trick to this?"

"No idea. Never been in a position where I've had to ask." They were a series of bumping limbs as Owen tried to release them. "We're shut in."

"Shut in? What kind of construction is this?"

"A stationery cupboard."

Sheepishly, Jason rubbed his nape.

"Mary," Owen said through the door, "get Jane." A small bark followed.

Silence fell thickly and Jason grabbed at straws to break it. "So. Mary. Who thought that up?"

"Me."

He'd expected a laugh. Some amused commentary on how such a name had come about. Because it wasn't common, was it? To name a dog with a ubiquitous woman's name? Owen was staring right at him, seemingly awaiting his response. Jason nodded soberly. "Oh. Actually, it's about time dogs had more respectful names. Nothing worse than a dog with a name like Paw-casso."

"It's short for Mary Puppins."

"Have I told you how much I like your uniform? The buttons. The pretty insignia. The whole thing." He stroked the fabric over Owen's chest in an attempt to pacify, then remembered the no manhandling rule and continued the motion an inch from his blazer. "Very smart. Very dry."

Owen shook his head. His expression had, over the course of the interrogation, steadily shifted right on the scale of disbelief, and Jason wasn't sure it could slide any more.

Light poured into the closet. Halleluiah. Saved.

Blinking, Jason twisted toward Jane, who was taking the

two of them in with a snorty laugh. "I don't even want to know what this is about."

Jason stepped out and Owen emerged after him, gulping in freedom.

"Thank you, Jane," Owen said, then checked his watch and turned to Jason. "The store opens soon."

Jason watched Jane retreat and then slid his gaze back up to Owen's. "You're letting me go? You won't tell anybody?"

"Let's resume this chat later."

"Like, here, or . . .?"

"My place. Or yours. As you wish."

How would that conversation go? A stern warning and a timeframe before Owen spilled the beans?

Jason bobbed his head, throat tight. "Yours. Definitely yours." He wasn't sure what Carl had lying around that might get him into trouble. More trouble. He paused and looked up into dark eyes. "Er, would this be an inopportune time to ask for a ride back later?"

"Inopportune?" There was a smirk there. A definite smirk. Maybe his word-choices had contributed to the cop's suspicion? He'd thought he'd been working his vowels just right. But accent wasn't everything, was it?

"I'll swing by the store and pick you up. But before you go, you need to remove your clothes."

Earnest Point Police
@earnestpointcops

Went out in the woods today and was sure in for a surprise! Lost teddy bear seeking his owner. He's told me I have to feed him honey cookies until he gets picked up from the station.

Chapter Four

"My . . . My clothes?" Jason gaped at Owen, who raised a brow, and then shook his head firmly.

"You're soaked, *and* shivering." He sauntered off and returned with a duffel bag. "I always keep spares for the gym."

Jason gazed down Owen's well-built length. The gym made sense—

Suddenly he was being turned around by the shoulders and escorted outside. "Better idea, change at the shop. You'll get wet dashing there anyway."

He let him go and Jason jogged across the road with the duffel, glancing back to see Owen planted under the awning, pointing him in the right direction—around a slight bend and across the road to Earnest Point Convenience Store.

Carl's corner store was like most corner stores. A refrigerated drinks and dairy section, bread and cereal aisle, junk food, bathroom and kitchen products, and three wide aisles of petware, everything from litter to shampoo to dog houses.

It was a bright space, crammed with colour, and Jason—cuddled into Owen's large hoodie behind the easy-to-manage till—was confident the job would be breezy.

Oh, shit. The pies. He was supposed to heat them up.

And that freshly-baked-goods delivery should have already arrived. What did he have to do if it didn't come? Bake himself? The staffroom barely had a functional kettle.

The storm raged outside. Customers anytime soon seemed unlikely, so he called Carl, who picked up with an upbeat "Howdy."

Practical concerns fled from Jason's mind. "You didn't tell me everything about Owen."

"Mostly everything."

"You said you barely saw one another."

"We barely do. Just the occasional ticket."

"I got the feeling you're rather infamous at the station."

"Well I *might* have been the subject of a tweet or two . . ."

A tweet or two . . . Jason made a mental note to look into that little gem later. "Expand on 'mostly everything'. What didn't you tell me?"

A pause. Jason imagined Carl shrugging. "I mean, we're neighbours. And we . . . went out on a date once?"

A startled zap had him doubling his grip on the phone. "You . . . He's . . . You're saying he *doesn't* have a pregnant wife and two dogs at home?"

"Huh?"

Sergeant Owen Stirling Sir was attracted to . . . "Then he has a husband and two dogs."

Unless he was attracted to men *and* women. Maybe there *was* a pregnant wife at home after all?

"What are you on about?"

This was all about general understanding, clearly. "Just crafting a mental picture of him." After a pause, he felt the need to add, "As I've done for *everyone* close to you in town."

"We're hardly close." Carl harrumphed. "Fine. Owen lives alone. Think he had a tough breakup about a year ago, when the boyfriend was about to move in. And, honestly, I don't know. I reckon I've seen him reading?"

Reading. That was an image right there. Owen rooted to a chair in a sunroom, eager fingers flipping the pages of a novel. Mary lying over his socked feet.

He nodded and nodded, and . . . "When did you, ah, hook up with him?"

"Hook up? God no. Haven't even kissed. It was just one date. Years ago. Before Pete."

"One date?"

"Our personalities didn't mesh. We both knew it. Since then, we've sort of avoided one another. He seems as annoyed as I am that I always land tickets. Or bike fines. Or get caught with a beer in a public place—you know. I might have a problem with rules."

"Rules, and preparing me for this mammoth favour I'm currently doing for you."

"Hey, don't deny part of you wanted this too."

The image of Cora in red, waving from the road, robbed his breath. "Be that as it may, it would've helped to know more about Owen."

"How so?"

"Maybe understanding how he ticks would've helped me keep this secret from him?"

The line crackled. "Owen *knows*?"

"I couldn't lie to a cop." Jason corrected, "I couldn't *keep* lying to a cop. He'd clearly figured it all out."

Carl swore. "How?"

Jason checked out the ceiling, wincing. "Not sure."

Carl's voice broke, "That's it, then? This is all over?"

Sickly disappointment wormed in Jason's middle. He cuddled deeper into Owen's spare hoodie, given to him—along with a spare T-shirt and shorts he had to scrunch up at the waist—so he wasn't stuck in wet clothes all day.

Was this all over? He hadn't realised just how important it was until he'd felt the impact of his mother's wave at Owen, the smile she'd tossed *him*. Who was this person who owned half of his face? Smiled like he did? He'd only just got here. He hadn't had a chance . . .

He stared determinedly out of the rain-drizzled windows toward the crossing, and then the station at the foot of a beech-studded hill. A curious energy rose within. "This is not over yet."

Mundane shop-related questions followed this pronouncement, along with a reminder to open the door behind the counter regularly to keep the nook from getting mouldy. Just as Carl hung up, the baked goods delivery arrived using said back door, so . . . two birds with one stone. At least something was going right.

Jason set the two-dozen glazed donuts behind plastic panelling near the bread section, admired his handiwork, then picked up his phone again and opened Twitter.

Figuring out what might be referring to Carl was tricky—naming and shaming was evidently not something the Earnest Point cops were into. Although, more than one "could the owner of this bike please collect it from the station and stop parking it on the cycle lane bollards" was accompanied by a photo of the mountain bike that lived in Carl's garage. Far more of Owen was revealed in these tweets than of Carl—in every third image he was helping some person or some creature or clearing up some problem. Helping elderly folks with storm prep, wrapping injured wildlife up in towels, posing with a class of schoolkids, settling a cuddly bear into an office chair—wait, what?

Anyhow, the man in these pictures didn't look the sort to push something over if someone might get hurt as a consequence.

A few minutes of scrolling made it clear, though, that whatever Carl had been up to, it probably wasn't that bad. Not that much of Earnest Point's criminal underbelly was especially nefarious. *Hil*arious, more like.

By the time the bell over the door jangled to signal a customer, Jason was giggling more than he had in a long time. The things the cops got called out to in this town . . . hastily, he turned on the alerts so he'd never miss a laugh, and spun to face the door.

It was Owen's nephew, from the station. He dripped his way inside and Jason grinned.

"Alex!"

Alex looked over, startled. "Hi, Carl."

Jason watched Alex grimace as he pulled a wad of money from his pocket, and went over to him, wiping his hands of icing sugar. "What're you after?"

"Dog food. I wanted to drive into the city but my car gave in down the road."

"I had a spot of car trouble this morning too." Alex counted the cash in his hand carefully, and Jason . . . understood. Being a student was tough.

Alex looked at him, tired and miserable. He was shorter than his uncle, and had a narrower frame, but Jason could see brief glimpses of Owen in the nose and the brow. Owen if he was much younger. Owen if he'd had a damn hard day.

Alex gripped his cash like he was afraid it might slip and be lost for good.

"Actually, we have half-off dog food today."

He led the way to the appropriate aisle and helped Alex carry a giant dog food bag to the counter. He rang it up and handed over the change. "Will you need a hand getting this home?" Or to Owen's? Mary was his, right?

Alex shook his head. "I live just up the road. The car was just for getting to polytechnic and work. I'll just have to figure something else out . . ." Alex flung out a half-baked laugh, but Jason sensed the stress behind it.

"I'm sure your uncle would give you a lift?" He knew this to be true. The protective aura was thick around that Sergeant Owen Sterling Sir.

Alex bit his lip. "I can't, y'know? He already does so much for me . . ."

"He does?"

He wasn't sure if that was supposed to be a question or a confirmation. He kind of felt like it had to be a fact, but Jason had always been nosy and Owen had become an important puzzle to solve. Especially if Jason were to convince him not to tell anyone the truth.

"Probably would've dropped out of school if not for him studying with me every day. He helped me get into polytech, and that's . . . He's just always giving up his time to me and Mum, especially since Dad left."

Alex blushed and stared at the dog food. He looked like he wished he hadn't said quite so much.

"Here's an idea. Borrow my Jeep while yours is out of action."

Alex stared, dumbfounded. "What?"

Wasn't this what small towns were all about? Lending a helping hand and all that? Owen had helped Jason out just this morning. "Yeah. Borrow my Jeep. I'll ride with your uncle."

"Are you serious?"

"Yes, absolutely." Jason paused and snuck in a cheeky smile. "I mean, there's a catch."

"Catch?"

"It needs . . . a little cleaning."

JASON SAGGED INTO THE PASSENGER SEAT OF OWEN'S CAR, tucking a few bags at his feet. What a day. That his ruse hadn't been discovered by anyone else was a miracle. How was he supposed to know Catbernet was a thing? It was logical he'd pluck a *cabernet* off the shelf and start spouting nonsense about how wild the grapes were with last year's local vintage. The patron had wanted it for their *missy*, but it would've been helpful to know Missy was a cat, not the beleaguered 'wifey' of a misogynist.

He dropped his head back and slowly turned his gaze to Owen.

Such a relief, to see a familiar face. A face that *knew* the real deal. Someone with whom he didn't have to worry about his accent slipping . . . Bliss. Even if it was only temporary. Even if tonight's conversation didn't yield the results for which he'd spent the day workshopping.

Jason smiled lazily, and Owen, still in uniform and as neatly pressed as this morning—*and* by some mysterious feat still smelling amazing—started the engine.

"We need to make a stop on the way home." Jason pointed down the street, fingers flashing in front of Owen's face.

Owen side-eyed him with a flicker of long lashes. "Hello to you too."

Jason grinned.

An arm around the back of Jason's seat, Owen backed swiftly out of the parking spot. His gaze dropped to Jason's attire—*his own* attire—like he'd forgotten he'd lent it out. Or maybe he saw a splosh of grease on it from that earlier incident with a mince pie?

"I'll wash this tonight and get it back to you tomorrow."

Owen turned his attention toward the street. "No rush. Where are we headed?"

"Alex's."

"Alex's?" Owen nearly stalled the car.

"Your nephew's, yes."

"Why?"

"He mentioned his mum was working a night shift, so I invited him to dinner. At your place."

Owen rubbed his jaw. "Let me get this right. Sometime in the eight hours since I last saw you, you've befriended my nephew and invited him to be picked up and driven to my place—a place you've never set foot in yourself, I might add—where you are planning on making dinner?"

All a bit presumptuous, put that way. "I was thinking he'd feel more comfortable at yours? But if you promise not to snoop around Carl's, we can all do dinner there."

"I wasn't aware we'd be doing dinner at all."

Jason simply hadn't imagined the evening *without* them eating together. He had fretted over the particulars all day, sure. But it'd still made sense that it would happen this way. "You live alone. I live alone. You want to *continue our chat.* And . . ."

A brow quirked.

"I'm sick of dinner for one."

Owen glanced at him.

Jason shook off the silly shiver that came at that flash of . . . pity? He laughed. "I'm even making dessert."

Owen slowed, letting an elderly woman weave around puddles on her way across the road. "Dessert. You're not trying to butter me up, are you?"

There was an intriguing idea. "Would that work?"

"No."

"Then I absolutely *won't* try it."

A bark had Jason catapulting in his seat, jerking against the belt and the arm Owen had instinctively thrown out.

Jason twisted to Mary Puppins in the back seat. "My intentions are good, you know."

Mary cocked her head. Jason prodded Owen eagerly on the shoulder. "Did you hear that?"

"What?"

"Nothing. Not so much as a squeak, so you *have* to believe I won't be trouble."

Owen pulled over, tooted his horn, and shook his head. "Oh, you're trouble all right."

TEN MINUTES LATER, JASON, ALEX, OWEN, AND MARY WERE filing through Owen's front door. Owen and Alex had each taken a bag off Jason, leaving him strangely empty-handed and feeling like a guest, which was odd, considering he'd initiated this whole thing. But a tingly-pleasant kind of odd. It made him want to laugh.

Alex dropped the groceries in a beautiful exposed-wood farm-house kitchen while Owen hesitated in the hall with his bag of Jason's rain-smelling clothes.

Oh, right. Jason stepped back into the hall and peeled off the hoodie, his T-shirt coming with it.

Paper rustled and the bag Owen had been holding thunked to the runner.

Jason dropped to his knees to collect the tangle of clothes spilling out of the bag. "I can be clumsy like that, too." He smiled up at Owen. A shaft of light fell over his blond hair and blazer and stopped at his belt. That massive belt. Quite hefty on his hips, surely. "How about we *both* get out of these clothes?"

When he didn't get a reply, Jason travelled his gaze up to Owen's face and found him scrubbing his jaw, eyes fixed on him. "I'm not quite sure *what* to do with you."

Jason's chest jumped. They were here already. The chat. He'd wanted to have this later, after dinner, after Alex had left, after Owen had seen Jason was harmless, really. The future of this ruse—the *decision* whether or not Owen would keep this to himself—was in Owen's hands. If he was willing, it could be safely ignored and forgotten. He'd even try hard to stay out of Owen's way. Plausible deniability and all.

Jason abandoned the bag and clasped his fingers together. His panicky voice got husky. "Do whatever you want to me, but keep this a secret, please. I'm begging you."

Owen's eyes flashed and he reached a hand to the top of Jason's head. Calming fingers in his hair. A stroke. A pet. Like he might do with Mary if she were anxious, or barking too loud.

Owen jerked back, startled, like he hadn't realised what he'd been doing. He strode off, hands clutched in his hair, groaning. "I need a shower."

Jason got to his feet as Alex joined him in the hall.

"What was that about?" Alex asked.

"I seem to be giving your uncle a bit of a headache."

"No way, nothing fazes him. He's as level-headed as they come."

Jason believed that. "Come on."

He tasked Alex with some food prep, jogged to Carl's, changed, and returned with a spare set of keys for the Jeep. Alex stopped grinning at tweets, took the keys graciously and migrated to the other side of the room, to the couch, where he and Mary could cuddle in front of *Home and Away*.

Dinner was simmering by the time Owen returned, barefoot in jeans and a soft-looking T-shirt. Wet hair dripped onto his shoulders and a pearl of water wove down the back of his neck. Quite instinctively, Jason swiped it away with a thumb as he passed.

"Hey, would you have an outdoor broom?"

Owen's fingers clasped his neck as he lounged against the

counter and took in Jason's tight jeans and tighter T-shirt. Jason figured at Owen's, he could leave the flannel behind.

"Don't have one at your place?"

Your place. Not Carl's. This careful wording around Alex was a good sign, right? Like Owen was willing to play along?

Jason shuffled closer. "Figured it'd be quicker to use yours than to search."

Owen left the room and came back with a sturdy broom. Jason took it, bounced it on its bristles, and called out to Alex, "Your transportation awaits."

Alex scrambled to his feet and took the broom with eager hands. "Thank you so, so much, Carl."

And off he went.

Jason smiled after him, then zipped back to the stovetop to make sure his risotto wasn't burning. When he looked up again, Owen was still where he'd left him, frowning in the direction his nephew had gone. "This day has been . . ." He gave Jason a perplexed look. "I've never had so many questions."

Jason stirred fresh apricots into the pan. "Alex is a great kid. Adult. New adult."

"From all your experience together?"

"You can tell these things right away. From the gentle way he speaks, and the way he talked about you."

"He talked about me?"

"There's something about his face, certain angles, *expressions*, where he looks like you, and I figure that comes from being brought up by you, and if he's been brought up by you, he's bound to be a good person."

Jason curled a finger for Owen to taste his risotto. He held out the wooden spoon and Owen eyed him over it. Steam wafted back in Jason's direction as he repeated, "If he's been brought up by me, he's bound to be a good person?"

"You came to my rescue last night. And this morning. And

maybe for the rest of the summer until Pete and Nick have tied the knot?"

Owen shook his head, laughing, and held the wooden spoon steady as he cupped his mouth around the end and tried. His eyes shut briefly and his throat jutted. "You can cook."

"I'll cook for you every night if . . . you'd like that. That's not a bribe, officer!"

A lazy yip came from where Mary sat, head on the back of the couch, watching them from between the cushions.

"Mary, please," Jason said. "I'll feed you too."

Owen laughed and made an umming sound in the back of his throat like maybe . . . maybe he was thinking about it? "Go back to explaining Alex's new transportation."

"I'm lending him Carl's Jeep until his is repaired."

A . . . rather stunned look.

"Alex didn't tell you his car broke down?"

"He mentioned it. Along with half-price dog food the likes of which the corner store has never had before."

"Oh, well . . . new promotion."

"I doubt promotions had anything to do with it."

Not so much, perhaps. But Alex didn't have to know that, and Jason hadn't minded balancing the till himself.

"He didn't mention the Jeep, though. Or your plan to feed us all."

"Such a solid guy, that Alex. He can totally keep a secret. Which I hope is something that runs in the family?" Jason gave his most winsome smile.

Owen rolled his eyes and moved to the window, peering into Carl's yard. Jason shifted alongside, trying to catch a glimpse of movement within the garage, too. They probably weren't searching for the *same* something.

A rumbled "I thought your Jeep had a problem?"

"Yes, one the size of"—Jason picked up Owen's hand, warm and gently calloused like his own. He spread those long, thick fingers apart on the windowsill, one by one, and wriggled more space between the thumb and forefinger. "That. But hairier."

Owen stared at his splayed fingers, then pressed his head against the glass with a heavy groan that seemed to vibrate along the pane and over Jason's skin. "I promised myself I'd never . . ."

Owen pulled back, squaring his shoulders. Carl's Jeep reversed out of the garage, but Jason's attention was fixed on blond hair and dark eyes and a decent shade of stubble . . .

The hand Jason had splayed to the size of the huntsman came up and landed on his shoulder, eliciting a shiver. *Not a spider.*

But the effect of it . . . a part of him had a strange urge to bolt. Only, Jason wasn't quite sure in what direction.

"I don't want you to leave."

Relief had Jason smiling widely. "You won't regret this. Promise."

Owen made a sound that said he was not at all assured.

Regardless, Jason was left with a hopeful taste in his mouth. Much better than dinner, or dessert.

After Alex took off with the leftovers, while Jason and Owen were cleaning up, Jason tried his best to explain why he was doing this, leaning heavily on Carl's motives rather than his own.

"Look, I respect your and Carl's decision, but I'm concerned someone will end up hurt."

"Someone was already hurting. That's why I'm here."

"There are others involved, too."

"Others who will only be hurt *if* they find out. Since you've kindly promised not to tell them . . ." Jason struggled to pull the plug on a sink full of water.

"There's still someone who'll be hurt if they don't. Maybe even especially."

Jason frowned, pausing his struggle with the slippery plug. "What do you mean?"

Owen plunged a hand into the water, catching on his own as he pulled. The wet glide of fingers and the sudden suction of water felt almost ticklish. He started to remove his hand and Owen tugged his thumb, casting him a sideways look. "*You*, Jason. If everything goes to plan, you're the one who leaves with no one knowing you were ever here. Ever the one making them laugh. Or cry, which I suspect is a definite possibility."

"I would never make anyone cry."

"I don't know. I was close to tears this morning."

"Well. I mean . . . tears of frustration don't count."

A shake of the head. "I've said my piece. There's only one thing I'd like to add."

"What's that?" Jason dried his hands on the tea towel hanging over Owen's shoulder.

"For God's sake, please just come to me in any wildlife-related emergency."

Jason laughed. "I'm sure I've had my quota. Bathroom?"

"Two doors on the left."

Jason didn't quite make it there. The first door on the left was open and there was a very large bed with the most impressive bookshelf-headboard. Just what kind of books did Sergeant Owen Stirling Sir read? Hardboiled detective stories? Cosy mysteries?

"What are you doing?" The voice came from behind, and Jason jumped out the three tip-toeing steps he'd taken into the master bedroom.

"Oops. Not the bathroom."

"No, it's not." Owen didn't seem annoyed. In fact, he seemed amused. He leaned against the doorframe, one ankle kicked over the other, arms folded. And waited.

It took about point-five seconds for Jason to tremble under the interrogative eyebrow arch. "Okay, okay. I'm . . . inquisitive. It's the Sagittarius in me."

Owen uncrossed his arms and stuffed his hands into his pockets. A wonder all that could even fit in the tight space. "The Sagittarius in you?"

"Adventurous. I like to explore."

"Explore," Owen repeated.

He looked *different* without his cop belt. "I'm all endless energy. Or, I'd *like* to be."

"And that's my limit of you for today." Owen came off the doorframe, clasped his shoulder, and Jason barely had the time to look up before he was being marched out of the house.

Earnest Point Police
@earnestpointcops

Finders keepers does not work on parked cars, people.

Chapter Five

J ason pulled his eyes away from the neat lines of glazed
donuts he'd arranged some minutes ago now. Once again,
he scanned the empty street on the other side of the
window.

Cora.

She'd be here any minute.

Owen had already fielded a barrage of questions on their
ride in this morning: what did he know about Cora, and was
she ever late for meetings, and what did he think about Jason
hugging her . . .

He wasn't sure he could, not without shaking. But maybe
she expected that?

He'd found it difficult to listen to Owen's responses over the
rampant pounding of his heart.

Now, the quiet store felt desperately still and silent, and he
nearly jumped out of his skin at a buzz from his phone. He
grinned at the latest police tweet: *Nobody told me policing would
involve dealing with so many inebriated kangaroos*. The image of calm,
practical Owen attempting to contain such a creature . . .
Immediately he imagined himself as that inebriated kangaroo,

bouncing the length of the store from junk food to dog houses, tackled to the floor by a tall, strong man in uniform. Sergeant Owen, come deal with him!

It was distracting at least, and if there was ever a time he needed distraction . . .

A flash of uniform caught his eye, and Jason was out of the shop and across the road in a flash.

"Christ."

"Er, sorry," Jason said, lurching to a stop in front of Owen. "Were you not on a break?"

"Just came from a noise complaint."

Jason looked around. "I don't hear anything."

Owen leaned in conspiratorially. "I'm good at my job."

"Mm. Probably why you figured me out quick."

"Cop or not, I'd have figured you out."

A laugh bubbled up Jason's throat, cleaving through his anxiety, and the shoulders he'd been tensing all morning relaxed. "What gave me away?"

"What didn't?"

"No, I mean, what was it *exactly*?"

"Two things, actually."

Jason made a nebulous hand gesture. "Well?"

Dark eyes twinkled, and Jason stepped closer, prepared for a whispered answer—

"Carl! Finally," came a cheeky voice from behind. "Thought you'd dropped off the planet."

Jason whipped around, recognising the tall figure with his auburn hair and freckled nose immediately. There'd been *so many* pictures of this guy on Carl's phone. At the beach, in the bush, piggybacking one another. Kissing.

The ex.

He needed to act cool. Totally at ease about the wedding. Moved on and everything.

Pete acknowledged Sergeant Owen Stirling Sir with a friendly nod.

Finally, Jason found his footing. "Pete. How ya doin', mate?"

Owen shifted behind him, clearing his throat. Jason made a mental note to correct his footing.

"Good. You've been quiet, yeah? Here I am trying to track you down about the party."

"What party?"

Pete laughed. "Yeah, yeah, it's my last big night out as an unmarried man. I know I go on about it."

A stag night? So soon? Jason scrambled to recall what Carl had said about it, and remembered only a downcast expression. He pinched his fingers apart and threw up a laugh. "Just a bit."

Owen moved again, and a breeze that had been chilling Jason's back disappeared.

Pete gazed over the road, where he'd left another familiar face. Nick, juggling two pups on leads. Softness filled Pete's eyes. Hell, if Carl was still half in love, watching *that* had to be torture. No wonder he'd begged Jason for this.

Pete turned back to him. "Bet you're looking forward to Angus."

Angus?

Jason gave a double thumbs up. "I am so looking forward to Angus." Owen made a low sound like a suppressed chuckle behind him.

Pete beamed. "Fab. Hey, I assume no plus one?" Before Jason could reply in the affirmative, Pete waved it off. "Of course not. So much on my mind—guests and table settings—not thinking clearly."

Pete laughed at his own nonsense and . . .

It hit a nerve.

Caroline with her fiancé. His empty home, the many nights

he'd spent awake, familiarising himself with each groan and creak of timber. Audiences applauding his renditions of Mozart and Chopin, coming up to him after concerts, but never speaking of anything beyond the music.

Pete's assumption he had no one reminded him he, in fact, had no one.

And yes, *Pete* was Carl's wound, but the root of it was the same wound. It stung. He wanted it not to be true, and he . . . he was here, in this small Australian town, given a chance to have something new. He was taking it.

Jason's smile ached. "I will need a plus one, actually."

Pete laughed.

"Something funny?"

Pete choked on that same laugh. It felt so good. The look of shock, so *satisfying*.

"You will? But . . ."

"I don't tell you everything anymore."

"Carl . . ." Pete suddenly cracked a grin. "You're having me on. Look, there'll be a couple of single guys at the wedding."

Another sting. Being called out making up a lie—even though it *was* a lie, *especially* because it was a lie—hurt. It hurt his pride, and the hot unfairness of it burned.

Pete continued, oblivious. "I'll introduce you."

Jason doubled down. Chucked out another laugh, like they were having a wee misunderstanding. "No-no. It's no joke. We've just been keeping things quiet."

Bewilderment. "Why?"

"Because . . ." Here Jason floundered a second, but only a second. "We didn't want to announce anything until we were serious."

"You're . . . serious?"

He clapped a hand on Pete's shoulder. "Ask yourself where I've been these last few days."

Pete opened his mouth and snapped it shut. It dropped open again.

"So if it's possible, I'd appreciate that plus one."

Pete stared at him, puzzled, like this possibility was so far from possible it was boggling his mind. "S-sure?"

Hold it in, Jason, hold it in—"He'll be coming to everything. The party. The wedding. All of it."

There'd been a steadily growing flurry of movement behind him and Jason could only imagine Owen internally groaning at this improvisation, folding his arms and dropping them on repeat. Maybe in an effort to resist knocking on Jason's noggin and asking what on Earth he was doing.

That would come later, no doubt.

"Who?" Pete asked.

For all Jason's impassioned outburst, he hadn't anticipated this very simple question. He faltered, stepped back on Owen's foot hoping he might provide a distraction to bail him out of this particular problem.

A soft *oof* fanned through the top of his hair and steadying hands gripped his hips.

Well. That wasn't very helpful.

Pete's frown deepened, and Jason blurted, "Oh my God, I reckon that's the pie timer!"

"Huh?" Pete pulled his gaze up. "I don't hear—"

Jason ripped himself out of Owen's grasp and jogged across the road (past Nick and pups), calling "We'll see you on Friday" behind him.

He ran straight to the fridges and stuffed his head into one, groaning. "So, that could've gone worse," he murmured. "You could've told him you're engaged."

A gasp startled him, followed by a lyrical voice. "Engaged?"

Slowly, he pulled out of the fridge and turned to an over-joyed grin and deep sparkling curiosity that quickly morphed to folded arms and a scowl. She batted a rolled-up magazine against his shoulder. "What haven't you told me?"

Jason stared.

Dark hair just like his, not a grey one in sight. Then, she'd only be forty. Cousin Cora. *Mother.*

He'd envisioned this moment all night, all morning, and none of his iterations had him *engaged*.

The doorbell chimed, and one glance had Jason's shoulders relaxing and his stomach knotting. A rather odd mix of relief and anticipation that he'd examine in more detail later.

Cora tapped the end of her magazine against his nose, laughing. "Don't keep me in suspense. Who were you supposed to tell you're engaged—*other than me?*"

God, he needed to untangle this mess.

In his peripheral vision, Owen halted in the junk food aisle just a couple of frantic bounds away. For a second, Jason wanted to bound over there, hide behind all that solidity and have Owen handle this for him.

He shook off the thought. "No-no, not engaged. I just . . . ran into Pete."

Cora scowled at the name, which spoke of the depths of her loyalty to Carl.

"Had to tell him I needed a plus one to his wedding, and he didn't take it great, and"—he gestured toward the fridge —"I was just contemplating how much *worse* it would have been if I'd had to tell him I didn't just have a boyfriend, but was also engaged."

"YOU HAVE A BOYFRIEND?"

Cora flung her arms around his neck and all his worries about this first hug were smothered. Soft warmth and hazelnut swallowed him whole. Nothing like the strong, quiet embrace his mum used to give him; this had its own flavour, a little hectic and immature. But full of love.

"You kept it quiet. You kept it *so* quiet. But I knew. You've been acting off these past weeks—I thought it was because you got landed being Pete's best man but . . . you were caught up in other feelings." She pulled back, her lipstick smudged, then yanked him close again. "Oh my God. It's in the stars. Whoever he is, he must be *the one*. Your horoscope's been predicting a love-match all month. Let's look."

Again, she pulled back, and wandered—with a wink and wave to Owen—to the counter.

Jason took a few seconds to gauge his bearings. He still felt the enthusiasm of her hug around him and . . . he didn't feel content like he'd imagined he would. Something painful lanced through him instead. His throat tightened.

That hug was for Carl, not for him.

He rubbed his brow and tried to chuckle the pang of jealousy away.

Owen had given up pretending to look at merchandise and was quietly observing him. He mouthed, "You okay?"

And that introspection, that clever cop intuition, that acknowledgement . . .

Heat stung behind his eyes; he nodded hurriedly and followed Cora to the counter.

"Capricorn." She read the horoscope—the *wrong* horoscope—aloud, and it did, in fact, predict a love match.

"What does Sagittarius say?" Jason murmured.

At her sharp look, he quickly added, "I'm on the cusp, Sagittarius feels more like me sometimes." *Always.*

"Sagittarius," she read slowly, a quiver in her voice. "You may have felt down and your love life completely non-existent, but your bright poise will soon pay off as someone with a kind and solid heart will show their interest in you. This is a love for keeps, but not one you'd usually consider. Be ready to open your heart to something special." She prodded both passages with a manicured finger. "See. They both say it—'a love for keeps'. So tell me *everything* about this boyfriend."

She bent lower over the counter, elbows on the glass, chin cupped in her hands.

Jason flustered and pinched the magazine. "Let me have a look at that."

He stared at the pages, words swimming, as he searched for something he could tell her. Specifics were out of the question at this point, and would be until he somehow found someone willing to play boyfriend for the rest of the summer.

He peeked over the top of the magazine and laughed at the cliché sight of Owen packing donuts into a box.

Cora cast a look over her shoulder at Owen too, and back to Jason with a funny eyebrow twitch. "You can't mean——"

Jason yelped at exactly where her thoughts had gone. "Look, I can't tell you much. He's, ah, wanting to tell his family first. Before the rumour mill gets started, y'know?"

"What about your family?"

"Oh, well. Um. We're going to invite both our parents to dinner sometime this week and tell everyone at the same time."

Cora glanced from him to Owen and back again, eyes narrowed in suspicion. And she was entirely wrong, of course, but . . . Owen might be the best option? Oh God, he'd been so magnanimous about this whole thing so far, would he . . .

Probably not. Surely that went too far, especially since he had an actual reputation to uphold around town.

Some Grindr random would be a better option. His stomach gave a sickly twist. He'd never been with a man, never so much as flirted with one. He wasn't sure he wanted to try acting close to a guy he'd never met, who might *expect* things in return.

He really had got himself into a pickle now.

There was, of course, the option of admitting he'd made the whole thing up, but . . . that made the twisting worse.

He'd just have to figure it out. Maybe Owen might know someone decent who was talented at fakery?

"Can I come?"

Jason pried his gaze off Owen and back to a smirking Cora.

"Come?"

"For the boyfriend unveiling."

"Ahhh." Owen approached with his donuts and a rather bemused expression. He raised a brow, awaiting what Jason would get himself into next. Good God, Owen had called it. He was trouble all right.

Jason nodded. Best he said nothing more on the boyfriend subject.

Cora clapped her hands, then stole the magazine back. "Hey, Owen?" she asked slyly. "What's your star sign?"

Owen set the donuts on the counter and fished out his wallet. "Libra. And I've never been so curious to have my horoscope read out to me."

He was smirking, and it was taking the piss out of Jason, but Jason couldn't scowl without his lips quirking. "I know what Libra's says."

Owen rested a hip at the counter and his twinkling eyes hit Jason's, daring him to go on.

"Libra. Someone absolutely fascinating has walked into your life and quite possibly turned it upside down, and though the temptation is there to make right all his messes, there's more adventure in letting them go."

Cora looked up, shaking her head. "Actually it suggests Libra be brave and not fear history repeating itself. *'This new chapter in your life, with much patience, might just have a most desired ending'.*"

Owen's smile stiffened, and he handed over his cash robotically. "Best not read too much into those."

Jason gripped the notes hard and watched Owen truck his purchases out of the store. What?

A little ache rose and fell. He wanted to chase after him, ask follow-up questions. Was *he* okay?

Jason caught Cora studying him, shaking her head in amusement. Gosh, she was going to be disappointed. Quickly, he swivelled the magazine around. "Let's read *yours*."

"Nope, can't actually hang today. I'm seeing Craig."

Craig rang a faint bell. Widower, accountant, two kids. "Fun date?"

"He wants to ask me something. Sounded serious!"

She rolled the magazine and tucked it under her arm, then raised her hand.

For a moment, Jason stared at her fingers. Then he snapped his own hand up and pressed their palms together in a wave, just like he'd practiced with Carl, but unlike anything he'd practiced with Carl. Little zings of *knowing* . . . Wondering what Cora thought every time she'd bid his brother goodbye like this . . .

His voice got croaky. "'Til the unveiling then."

Earnest Point Police
@earnestpointcops

Thinking of breaking the law?
Here's a better idea: Don't.

Chapter Six

The whole drive home, and throughout dinner—which Jason had gone ahead and cooked at Owen's again. Seriously, it was easier to cook for two, the company was superior, and splashing Owen with soapy suds during clean-up made for some excellent entertainment. He really had quite the unfathomable stare, dark pools that made you feel naughty indeed, and want to immediately chirp out an apology before doing it all over again.

Anyway, throughout all this Owen kept giving him this other look. Like he was waiting for—and fearing—the next outrageous thing Jason might do. The look was measuring, and he grimaced, as if afraid what the results might be.

Jason wanted to assure him he'd keep a steady head from here on out. No more wild lies that made this whole mess messier. But Mary was watching them with big eyes from the couch, and she'd yip for sure.

Owen looked at him expectantly.

Jason dried his hands on his T-shirt. The small step over to Owen and his shoulder-draped tea towel suddenly felt too nerve wrecking. Because . . . because they'd chattered about non-consequential things all evening, but Owen had been there today. He'd seen the wreck with Pete and then the punch that came with seeing his mother. Owen knew more than anyone else in this town. And, for that matter, in his entire life. A man he'd known only a couple of days.

You okay? he'd mouthed.

It made that small step between them feel raw and intimate, and Jason yanked himself a good step toward the door, laughing, jerking fingers through hair that should've been longer. "I, um, better . . ."

Owen slid the tea towel off his shoulder and hung it on the oven door. "You don't have anything you'd like to ask me?"

Jason blinked.

A thorough side-eye. "About what happened earlier?"

It hit him. The moment in the shop. The horoscope that had drained Owen's smile. "Y-you wouldn't mind if I just asked you?"

"Mind?" Owen hummed. "I'm not sure how I feel about it, to be honest. But I'm bracing for it, nonetheless."

Jason nodded sombrely and decided, nerve wrecking or not, this kind of delicate question required him crossing the raw and intimate space between them, touching Owen's soft-sleeved arm, and looking up into the unfathomable. "Owen?"

"Yes, Jason?"

His insides jolted. How strange to be so affected by the sound of his own name. Maybe because it felt dangerous to say it aloud, in case anyone overheard. That danger was scary.

And also . . . thrilling?

But enough getting lost in his own feelings. He wanted to understand Owen's. "Libra shouldn't fear history repeating itself?"

"*Libra* . . ."

If Jason had thought Pete looked puzzled at Carl having a

boyfriend, it was nothing to what was crossing Owen's face. He looked genuinely *perplexed.*

Had Jason been imagining Owen's quiet response at the store? No. He *had* been affected by that horoscope. Jason felt that to his core. Then this bafflement came from elsewhere—

Jason winced. "You were expecting a different question, weren't you?"

"In fact, I was."

Jason dragged his hand off Owen's arm with a sheepish smile and rocked back. "Can we just forget that I tried to ask you something probably very personal?"

Owen scrubbed a hand over his jaw and leaned back against the lip of the sink. "It's fine. My last relationship . . . wasn't the healthiest. I went into it in a delirious rush. I fell hard and fast, and it ended similarly."

"Right before he was supposed to move in?"

A heavy raised eyebrow.

Jason tried again with the guilty grin. "Um, Carl told me that part?"

"Tell you a lot about me, did he?"

Jason eyed the full spectrum of Owen's Oweness. A crazily chiselled cop with charm. "Trust me, he skimped on the details."

A laugh, bright and full-bodied, like the taste of a grape straight from the vine. It vanished in the space of a swallow, but the aftertaste lingered. And Jason wanted more.

Owen shifted, rubbing his nape. The juxtaposition between the laugh and this . . . Jason touched the tips of his fingers to Owen's arm again.

"Hayden broke up with me the day we were supposed to move in together."

"What spectacular timing."

"Hmm, but I've learned a lot about timing since then." He paused and said poignantly, eye to eye, like it was wisdom to be passed on, "It's a load of bollocks to fall in love at first sight."

Jason patted his arm. If he'd learned anything from his past relationships, it was that they took work. A lot of work. Finding instantaneous connection from the start? Myth. Hell, finding connection after years might be a myth too. "I feel the same way. Complete bollocks."

Owen took a long time searching Jason's face for sincerity. Jason was *one hundred percent* serious. Let Owen look, let him freaking *taste* the truth on the breath rising towards those quietly flattened lips.

Owen nodded and seemed to relax against the counter. "Ask your next question."

"Really? 'Cause I've been holding onto this one, um, since that moment on the street earlier."

A wry grin. "Quite the moment that was."

Jason gave his toothiest grin.

Owen rubbed his hands together and clapped. "Right. I'm ready for it."

"What were the two things that gave me away?"

JASON HADN'T THOUGHT OWEN WOULD STEER HIM OUT OF HIS home, once again groaning about having reached his limit.

It was all very efficiently done, a firm yet gentle grip on the back of his neck, steady steps, and disbelieving laughter—and Jason . . . sort of, kind of, completely got it.

Owen had *thought* he was ready to share, but had quite suddenly been overcome with embarrassment. Probably he'd been standing there, going over what he'd just disclosed about his ex, and wondering why he'd spoken about it at all. Wondering why he was inviting more questions. It was simply too much, too soon in their neighbourly relationship.

That was okay. Jason knew what it was like to say a little too much. Today, with Pete and Cora. Prime examples.

At least Owen quit while he was ahead.

But two things had given Jason away, and he couldn't have those same things giving him away to others. If Jason wanted Owen to share—and he did, desperately—he'd have to engage in more bonding. A lot of deep bonding that coaxed Owen into spilling.

Jason turned his gaze away from the view of Owen shaking his head and retreated to the other side of the fence. He fished out his phone and paced Carl's house as he looked up ways to bond with neighbours online. Halfway down a listicle—

What was he doing? Priorities! Cora and Pete—and no doubt by now most of Earnest Point—expected him to reveal his non-existent boyfriend. That's what he should be searching for. Someone to be his special someone.

Oh, and . . . oops. He called Carl. "Iaccidentallytoldevery-oneyou'reinasecretrelationship."

Carl remained silent. Stunned, probably. "Say what?"

"You have a special someone and you're taking them to the wedding."

"Oh my *God*."

"Pete got to me?"

"You're meant to *not* let him get to you. That's why you're there and not me." Jason imagined poor Carl gripping his hair, wishing he hadn't given Jason all his flannel so that he could use it to fan himself. "Oh *shit*." And Carl started . . . laughing.

Jason wasn't quite sure what kind of level of freaked out that made Carl. Um. "Don't worry? I have it all under control. I'll fake something then break up after the wedding. It'll all be dealt with before you return."

"You—you realise I'm completely gay, right? Not bisexual? That means—"

"A boyfriend, yeah. That's what popped out of my mouth in front of Pete."

"Christ."

"And Owen."

"I . . . just don't know what to say."

Jason winced. "And Cora."

Carl made a sound as if swallowing panic.

"She's so lovely, Carl. She was over the moon for you."

Carl sighed. "She's always wanted me to find someone solid; someone who I came first with. She'll be extra interested in whoever it is. You're really gonna have to know everything about him. You're gonna have to show he's someone worth keeping secret from *her*. So act super-duper in love, yeah? I can tell her later I got carried away and we weren't right for one another, but in the meantime, you've gotta act *crazy* in love."

Jason chuckled nervously.

Carl paused. "You've never had a boyfriend before, have you?"

"No?"

"You gonna be able to pull this off?"

Jason wasn't quite sure. But . . . Mary wasn't here, so —"Oh, absolutely. No sweat."

"You might actually have to kiss him in public to make it look real. I'm into PDA."

"Ha, right!" Beads of sweat were forming at his neck; they tickled as they slid down, echoing in a little quiver deep in his belly. "Anyway, I gotta go and . . ." *download Grindr to fish out a good match for this.*

"Yeah."

"Yeah."

"Oh, and Jase? Could you, pretty please, not call with any more surprises?"

Carl didn't have the Grindr app, which, okay. Bit of a relief, really. So Jason spent the next hour installing it, setting up a profile, and panicking in the shower. There were so many guys on there, so many terms he'd had to look up, and so many *images* that came with them. It was all very . . . overwhelming. He wanted someone safe to pretend with, someone who would enjoy a bunch of events because it came with free food and booze. Not someone who wanted to be milked by a twinky showoff with an uncut dick.

Didn't everyone around here have an uncut dick?

A hoard of images popped into his mind—not at all helped by his internet searching. Those acronyms all needed decoding, after all. The images had come entirely unprompted.

He snapped the water to cold, then stood shakily on the mat. Right. He should . . . probably get to the messaging part of things.

He dripped his way to the bedroom, shoved on boxers and a loose sleeping T-shirt, a little on the threadbare side, but perhaps the semi-translucent quality would make an appealing picture? Better than the temporary one of a puppy he'd put up there, probably. He had no abs, but he did have a nice flat stomach, and his frame tapered to the waist—so as long as the T-shirt kept things vague, he'd look desirable. Ish?

He groaned and flopped onto the piano stool, staring desolately at his phone.

The piano tinkered, tuneless notes and keys dipping to a ghostly touch. Jason jumped to his feet and peered into the open piano. He jerked back with a shriek, and it grew.

"SERGEANT OWEN STIRLING, SIR!" He yelled it as he raced through the house, and then again as he hopped barefoot over gravel, and then again as he hightailed it up Owen's path. "PLEASE, *I NEED YOU.*"

Owen whipped open the door, awash with concern, a toothbrush clenched in one hand, a splotch of white across his lip. Boxers and a loose T-shirt of his own, and all those muscles. Made for protection. Made for—

Jason—convinced the very, very slithery snake he'd just seen had chased him and *was still* chasing him—jumped into Owen's arms and climbed as high as he could possibly get. "Shut the door! Quick—"

Owen had dropped his toothbrush in the process, but he'd caught Jason around the thigh, the knee, immediately taking his weight. A firm pressure guided him around his waist, then skidded to the small of his back, between his shoulder blades. The heat of splayed fingers burned, like a shield, and hips cocked to keep Jason perched, a supportive pressure under his arse. Jason shuddered and tightened his legs around Owen. Shaking arms curled behind that blond head. "Don't put me down, please, *please.*"

"Okay, Jason. I've got you." The door closed. "I've got you." Thumbs rubbed against his back and serious eyes met his. "What's going on?"

Mary had come to check out the chaos and clearly didn't sense his fright. Not a yap to be heard, nothing but padding paws and a waggling tail. Like somehow this scene pleased her. Karma coming for him after all his lies? Oh God, maybe he did deserve this.

Jason convulsed with more shivers. "I'll just live with you, okay? It's only a few weeks. I just . . . you're so calm and steady and strong and you can deal with all *this.*"

A light chuckle, and a tightening grip. "Deal . . . I don't know about that."

Right, Jason hadn't exactly given him context. If he'd just stop panicking, he could spit it out.

Owen hitched Jason up further and moved into the living room. The motion sent gravity slithering through him like a snake of his very own. He ducked his head to Owen's neck, hugging him close. "How do you manage it?"

"What, sweetheart?"

"The vicious pounding of your heart just at a *glance.*"

"Mmm, not well."

"It's the first time I've ever . . ." *Snake, snake, snake.* The word wouldn't pass his tongue. "I'm freaking out."

"I'm right there with you."

"No, *you* can't freak out. I need you to be the one to tell me what to do! To make it all better."

Owen said nothing to that, just settled him gently onto the couch. Jason wasn't ready to unlock his arms though and Owen was left no choice but to collapse atop him. Heavy, warm armour that encased him from head to toe. "Can I stay under you forever?"

Owen expelled a breath that funnelled over the top of his hair.

Mary padded to the armchair beside them and curled up, and . . . he liked Mary around too. She would certainly let them know if there were a snake or any other unwanted wildlife inside. "You, me, and Mary. The three of us together."

"Christ, Jason." That deep gravelly voice vibrated through the very thin material trapped between them. "Do you ever listen to yourself?"

Jason let his head sink back on a cushion that Owen had fed under him. "Sorry." He didn't handle panic or fear well. He took a deep breath and loosened his hold on Owen.

Owen rose just enough to look him in the eye. Dark depths, and something lurked there . . . Something that made him want to jump, just like—"I've never seen a snake like that before." He hadn't seen *any* snake before, except for that one at the zoo. "It was bigger and longer than I'd imagined they could be, and its eyes shone like . . . like it wanted me."

Owen's mouth twitched at the corners. "I'll help you." He pulled himself off Jason, grabbed his phone, and turned his whole body towards the window overlooking Carl's.

He made a call to a snake catcher. He organised the when, the where, the how. Jason watched the taut lines of Owen's back as he shifted. The way they flexed when he laughed, when he confirmed the schedule, when he said cheers. Calm and clear. What would it be like to have that sort of practical confidence?

Jason heard a dull click and looked down at his hand, surprised to find himself still gripping his phone. He hadn't been aware of it as he bolted over here, but apparently it had fused onto him with his fear, and he'd just popped the cover off. He fixed it and pulled the folded blanket from the back of the couch over his goosebumped limbs.

"Steve will be right over. I've used him a couple of times for a tiger snake and a lowland copperhead. He'll move them down the hill." Instead of coming over to Jason, Owen tucked himself behind the kitchen island and began brewing them tea. Jason had to tip his head over the arm of the couch to see him. "You may want to check there are no gaps in your doors or screens."

"Um . . . yeah, I was serious." Another shiver punctuated his point. "I don't think I can go back there tonight."

Owen paused, a spoon hovering above the honey jar, then slowly dipped it inside. "I have a guest room."

"Can Mary sleep with me?"

"Mary?"

"Or you." Kind and capable, right there. The perfect presence to help Jason relax. He'd be able to handle anything. Everything. "I'd *love* to sleep with you."

Owen looked up sharply. "You can have Mary."

THEY DRANK TEA UNTIL STEVE KNOCKED ON THE DOOR AND HE and Owen—who'd changed into sweats—headed over to Carl's to deal with the cold-blooded intruder.

When Owen came back an hour later, Jason was still on the

couch, scrolling through Grindr with Mary curled at his side. He'd widened his search to include three bigger towns nearby, desperate to find a profile that didn't freak him out.

"Done," Owen said. "What are you frowning at?"

Jason smacked his lips on the taste of honey and waved his phone. "Grindr."

Owen tripped over the edge of the rug and caught himself on the coffee table. He peered at Jason's screen. "Why?"

"I don't know what half these acronyms mean."

"I meant *why are you on Grindr?*" Owen perched on the arm of an adjacent chair, something very cop-like in the way he folded his arms and studied Jason.

Jason straightened under the scrutiny, a tiny little electrical frisson in his gut, like . . . like he'd been caught in a lewd act. "It isn't obvious? I need a fake boyfriend."

"*That*'s where you're looking for a fake boyfriend?"

"Do you have any better ideas?"

Owen stared at him, lips parting—maybe to reply—but no words escaped. Then he frowned and cast his gaze away. "I . . . hope you know what you're doing."

"Not in the slightest. I just downloaded the app tonight and it's all very *much*."

"You *just* downloaded . . ." like he wasn't sure he'd heard correctly.

"I hate this." Jason sighed. "Here's a genius idea. Maybe you could help?"

Owen shook his head, laughing gruffly, then scrubbing his jaw. "*Now* you ask?"

"I might've asked earlier if you hadn't marched me back to Carl's."

"I marched you over there because I expected *this* to be the first question out of your mouth this evening."

"You expected me to ask for help finding a fake boyfriend on Grindr?"

Owen's eyes doubled back to his and his hand stilled over his lips and chin. Then he groaned, and groaned again as he stood and marched out of the living room. "Guest bed is the room next to mine. Good night, Jason."

"Wait, where are you going?"

"To vent my frustrations."

"That sounds . . . like something I might read on Grindr."

A door shut solidly.

❧

JASON TOOK MARY WITH HIM TO THE GUEST BEDROOM AND snuggled into the bed, propped against the headboard with pillows, the light from his screen beaming towards his face. Left swipe. Left swipe. Left swipe.

A notification.

Jason clicked. The profile pic was a generic closeup of two men's hands interlocked. A guy who liked handholding. Promising.

Twenty-nine. Looking to start out as friends. Would eventually be interested in LTR (long term relationship). Safe: PrEP, regular testing. Top.

Jason couldn't see any distance on the screen, but if he was going to brave chatting up anyone, this would be the anyone to be brave with.

He wrote, and soon there was a series of yellow and blue bubbles.

Call Me Carl: Hey, nice profile.

Daniel: Puppy on a piano?

Call Me Carl: I was meant to change that, but I had an incident with a greedy-eyed snake.

Mary's head lifted off his lap, ears perking, and Jason paused his chat, freezing at the horrifying thought there was another slithery beast lurking nearby. Then he let out his breath and reclined against the headboard. Just Owen, shifting in his bed next door. Laughing at something.

What could he be reading that made him chuckle like that? Jason petted Mary. If only dogs could talk.

Daniel: No worries. What are you into?

Call Me Carl: Friends, sort of? I need a fake boyfriend for a few key moments over the next few weeks?

Jason gave the tl;dr shortened version of his predicament, and somehow, fifteen minutes later found himself agreeing to meet Daniel one town over in Mulburry the following day, for dinner at Trinity. Didn't Alex work at Trinity? Small place. No idea how he'd recognise Daniel, but he had instructions and an assurance they'd find one another.

Grinning, Jason dropped the phone to the bed and twisted onto his knees. He knocked on the wall he shared with Owen and called "I did it, Owen. I have a date! A real actual date with a guy."

Owen made a sound like a snort, followed by a sigh. "Get some rest. Tomorrow will be interesting."

Earnest Point Police
@earnestpointcops

For those who lost their bumpers today going thirty over the new speedbumps outside Sundale school: #schoolzone #slowdown #kidscrossing #newbumpers

Chapter Seven

"You know how I have a date this evening?"

"Yes, Jason. You mentioned it three times over breakfast." Owen had been wearing a bemused expression all morning, and it only deepened when he parked outside the local café. Owen's coffee machine had chosen that morning to malfunction, and Owen really, really needed the caffeine. He'd taken one look at Jason and said so himself.

Owen locked up and led the way inside.

Jason had barely slept from fretting about The Date. He must look wrecked from all that tossing and turning. More unkempt than Mary loping behind them, one ear cocked over her head, yawning.

Oscillating between incredible relief, excitement, and crippling fear of what was to come, he kept rubbing his palms over his jeans over and over. If he wasn't careful, he'd be attending his date with holes covering the length of his thighs. Right now, his stomach was dancing.

As they waited for their order, Owen's gaze dropped to Jason's hands and his expression did cop-like things. Gosh, no hiding anything with him.

"So the thing is, would you be able to drop me off in Mulburry? Or should I ask Alex if he's working?"

"I happen to be heading there too."

"What a coincidence."

Owen spared him a look he couldn't quite interpret, but it zinged as he tried.

Jason did that thigh rubbing thing again, and Owen paused. "It's not a real date. Why are you so nervous?"

Takeaway cups slid across the counter into Owen's waiting hands, then on to Jason. A short walk later the wind was a lazy caress as Owen led him and Mary over a stone wall into sand and tussock. They sipped their coffee while Mary loped through sunny patches behind them, and watched waves crest over a smooth shore.

Owen lifted his cup and blew carefully on its near-boiling contents. His eyes held Jason's expectantly, and Jason took a burning sip of his own. "I know it's not real, but there's part of me that's curious."

"Curious?"

"And freaked out. I've never been out with a guy before."

Owen froze, cup to his lips. "You've never been out with a guy before?"

"Mmm. Even in a faking-it capacity, I don't know what to do or how to act." He kicked his leg out, spraying sand. "I never so much as flirted with a guy."

Owen choked and coffee sprayed in an impressive arc over his lap.

He coughed.

Jason patted his back.

"You okay?"

Owen took a few more seconds to clear his airway, then immediately cocked his cup for another gulp. "That was the last thing I expected."

"My brother's gay so you assumed I liked men too?"

"I certainly assumed you liked men."

"Part of me wants to get haughty and deliver a scathing line about assumptions, but . . ." Jason laughed at himself. "Sometimes I wonder what it would be like?"

"Curious."

"A bit." Getting that tiny morsel of a secret off his chest had him sagging into his seat. It didn't seem quite so big anymore.

Scratch that. He still had a fake date this evening, and he'd be even more hyperaware of himself then, imagining what it would be like if it were real . . .

Jesus, as if things weren't challenging enough.

He should push curiosity aside. Focus on the plan. A fake boyfriend to rub in Pete and Nick's faces and prove 'Carl' was totally emotionally together. And quite the catch.

Owen watched the waves, the horizon, face crunched in disbelief. He let out a dry laugh and the edges of his eyes gently creased. "You certain you haven't so much as flirted?"

Jason started to shake his head and stopped, blood draining from his face. Mortification refilled it. "OMG, that call! Carl just thrust his phone into my hand and I panicked. Apparently I get husky when I panic, and I really, really panicked."

"Makes sense."

"That I got unintentionally husky?"

"That it was you on the phone."

"Sorry about that." Jason bit his bottom lip in the rhythm of Wagner's "Flight of the Valkyries". "Did you, uh, already suspect something was off then?"

"Not then." A sideways glance with twitching lips and fingers drumming on a coffee cup. "When you arrived and scared yourself shitless in the hall mirror."

"It was a kangaroo," Jason said emphatically, and Mary had to go and bark behind them. He scowled into another sip of caffeine. "Can't get away with anything, can I?"

"I wouldn't say that." Owen finished his coffee and gestured back towards the car. "About your date this evening . . . You'll do just fine."

"Reckon I'll be convincing enough?"

"Yes." Laughter. "Scarily so."

DURING THE QUIET HOURS AT THE SHOP, JASON DITHERED about straightening things to the Australian Symphony Orchestra playing Beethoven's *Fidelio*. Music kept his thoughts from drifting to the evening, kept him in the here and now. Focused on lining up the Catbernets. Neat. Neat and clean. Unlike himself thanks to a wee accident with a frosted cream donut.

Crap, he couldn't turn up to his date in these clothes . . . also, would Carl really wear flannel to a date? Maybe he could get away with a button-up and some cashmere, just this one time? He'd have to get Owen to swing past home first, of course—

A tap on his shoulder.

Jason swung around so fast his earbuds fell out of his ears to hang around his neck. The first thing he noticed was the smile—warm and familiar, so much like his own and Cora's but set in a weathered face, more crinkled with age. Great Aunt Patricia, or 'Mum' to Carl.

"Thought I'd pop in, darling," she said.

Jason snapped out of his stare and affected a laugh. "Sorry, got caught up in my head."

That smile grew and she gestured him behind the counter, where she perched on his seat with a grateful sigh. "Thinking of a special someone, were you? Hmm?"

Eerily close. "Um . . ."

Jason didn't know what to do with his hands or his feet. He

shifted his weight around, leaned forward with his elbows on the counter, straightened again.

"Look at you. Terrible at hiding the truth."

Jason gulped.

She raised her hands. "Okay, guilty. Your cousin came around yesterday and spilled the beans about the new boyfriend."

"Oh." All these monosyllabic noises. He had to think up something better to say.

A laugh. "We can't keep any secrets."

"Can't you?"

Abort, abort. Totally the wrong thing to say. All that attitude!

Patricia's laughter came to an abrupt halt. "What was that, darling?"

Uhhh. "If you can't keep secrets, I can't tell you who he is yet." He gave her a naughty-naughty finger waggle.

The frozen look in her eyes melted and the laughter resumed, the quality of it more relieved than humoured. "When's this unveiling, then? Tomorrow I hope."

Jason sighed deeply when she left. Well that went . . . it could have been worse.

His cell phone chimed, a welcome distraction from the strange mix of feelings in his stomach.

Pete: after work adventure! Late night shopping. Let's drive to the city and pick up our
suits

Jason: Sorry, mate. Got a date

Pete: Can't you shift it?

He probably could, but . . . 'Carl's' life didn't revolve around his ex, and Pete would have to get used to that. Also,

Cora and 'Mum' were expecting an unveiling, like, tomorrow, and first Jason had to meet Daniel and be sure this fakery would work. And finally, he just . . . didn't want to shift it.

Jason: Sorry. Won't have time tonight

The dots moved on the screen for a long time before Pete replied.

Pete: Looking forward to chatting with you both about . . . how this all happened

Jason bet he was. He'd grill the poor man to the brink of sanity. Maybe it'd be wise not to freak Daniel out about those specifics too early. Tonight would be making the fakery gig sound worthwhile.

Worthwhile. Jason swallowed. Would tickets to all his performances in Australia or New Zealand for life be a welcome suggestion? Or was that thinking too green?

He found himself texting again.

Jason: What do I offer this guy? To convince him to be my fake boyfriend?

Owen: I wouldn't worry about that

Jason: If he asks me to milk anything, I might bolt, table around my middle

Owen: Lol. He won't

Jason: Okay, okay. Oh, btw, can we stop off home first? Need to dress for date

Owen: You look fine as you are

Jason: I frosted my pants

Owen: ?

Jason: They're all crusty. Delicious, I'm
sure, but he won't know that

Owen: . . .

∾

THEY DROPPED MARY OFF AT ALEX'S FOR THE NIGHT, AND
swung by home. Jason stopped with his key in Carl's door, and
swiftly backtracked to Owen pulling mail out of his letterbox.

"Thought you were desperate to change?" Owen said, flipping through his mail.

"Absolutely."

Owen peered at him.

Jason rubbed his nape. "I need you to come."

"Come?"

"Watch."

Owen rubbed the corners of three envelopes against his
brow. "Watch what?"

"That no snake tries to inject me with its poison."

"I'm sure all snakes will behave themselves."

"But what if there's something about me they're drawn
to?" Jason made a cursory sniff of his armpit. "What if they
emerge from their dark, damp crevices and come at me?"

Owen shut his eyes. "I'm going inside to change."

He strode toward his place and left the door open, which
Jason took as an invitation to follow along if he must.

Jason followed along and paced in front of the closed

bedroom door until Owen emerged, fresh and sculpted in a navy cotton button-down, light denim jeans and brown leather shoes. He hung a beaten brown leather jacket over his shoulder and met Jason's gobsmacked stare with a questioning stare of his own.

Jason laughed. "It's always an adjustment, seeing you out of uniform. Say, are you in any of those charity calendars? You know, Mr July?"

"Mr July," Owen repeated deadpan.

"A winter month for sure." Jason gestured vaguely toward . . . all that. "Heat 'em up and everything." A pause. "You must be doing something nice this evening."

"Nice. Torturous."

"Is it . . . dinner with the parents?"

"Parents?"

Jason tried on a . . . smiling grimace? Or something that looked appropriately sorry and not sorry? He tagged behind Owen towards the front door, where he collected his keys and wallet. Phone. "Alex came into the store today, he needs the Jeep another few days. We got to chatting and when I said you were driving me into Mulburry, he said it's probably because you were seeing Nanna and Pop, who I assume are your parents?"

Owen paused, staring at his screen. "Yes, well. Doubt I'll be seeing them any time tonight."

Right. They'd both be late if they didn't get moving.

Jason grabbed hold of Owen's forearm, soft light hairs tickling his palm, and tugged him over the threshold. "Be my personal watchman while I dress. Promise I'll be quick."

Jason tried to keep his door closed as he changed, but a creak from the vicinity of the bed had him tripping over the baggy jeans he'd been stripping out of and flinging open the door.

Owen—who kindly, patiently, waited in the hallway gazing

at the ceiling from his position propped against the wall—glanced at Jason's flurried commotion. Something flashed across his face, but Jason had known him long enough now that he could dismiss it as surprise. In fact, as quick as the flicker in his eye had come, it settled again. An air of *I expected something like this* was coming from him now.

Jason stomped out of the jeans and, casually as he could, thumbed over his shoulder. "I, ah, might need you to peek into dark places?"

Owen graciously swept into his room—a little smirk at his lips—and thoroughly investigated the underside of Carl's bed.

"All clear."

Jason had yanked his tightest jeans on in the meantime—that way, if something got free, maybe the denim and his socks would be an impediment.

He shrugged his shirt on and paused. "I swear I heard something."

"It's an old bed and an older house." Owen's eyes slipped down to Jason's stomach, where—oh hell, he was poking buttons into the wrong holes. Owen cleared his throat.

Jason undid the buttons and started over, glancing at the *old bed*. He should have considered this. He owned a 1905 villa for crying out loud. "My wood groans too."

Owen jerked his eyes up.

Jason absorbed all that dark-eyed curiosity and smiled. "Yes, I have my own home and my own life—and it's quite different from Carl's. Although, we've obviously both got groaning wood that needs tending to."

Owen walked out of the room. Just turned and swept out.

"Owen?"

A grumble came around a bend in the hall, unintelligible.

Jason finished the last of his buttoning, grabbed his wallet, stuffed his feet into his nicest sneakers and raced after him.

~

Jason thought he'd park somewhere in the town centre and they'd go their separate ways, but Owen pulled up close to Trinity and strode alongside him to the doors.

Jason halted. In all his talk of his date tonight Owen hadn't asked which restaurant he was meeting Daniel at, and Jason hadn't mentioned it either.

He rang out an amused laugh. "Don't say you're having dinner here."

Owen opened the door and beckoned him inside. "I'm having dinner here."

"What are the odds!"

Owen pinned him with quite the expressionless look. "Inevitable, really."

Jason frowned. Then nodded. Small towns. Of course everyone would know everyone and bang into everyone, and eat dinner at the same restaurant, too. He entered the pretty establishment—high ceilings, beautiful coastal artworks, and a pleasant kind of light that made patrons look fabulous—and Owen slid next to him.

None of the tables hosted any lone men. Daniel mustn't have arrived yet.

"Owen?" He twisted and looked up at him. "Do I look . . . okay?"

"Okay?"

"Good enough he won't spot me and leave?"

Owen touched his shoulder, maintaining eye contact. "Why on earth would anyone do that?"

A light laugh flittered out of Jason, soft and sweet as a butterfly and reflected in Owen's smile. "I know it's fake, but I had the sudden fear he'd be expecting"—Jason swept hands up and down, encompassing all of Owen's Oweness—"more of *that*."

Jason stepped closer and plucked stray dog fur off Owen's sleeve.

Owen gave him a twinkly-eyed smile. "You look amazing, Jason." He dipped, and words skated over the tip of his ear. "Have a great fake date."

Owen drew back and Jason's skin kept tickling.

Someone behind them cleared their throat to hurry them along, and an approaching waitress gestured to the room and told them to sit where they pleased. Straightening himself, Jason flashed Owen a nervous grin. "Enjoy your dinner, too."

"I sure will."

Jason beelined to a free table. He started for one at the window, which would have given him a great overview of everyone coming into the restaurant, but then the grand piano in the corner caught his attention, and he swerved toward a table near that.

Gosh, Daniel had knocked it out of the park when he'd suggested this place.

He slid into a chair, gazing at the beautiful instrument bereft of a musician, and wondered if he could just . . . No. Focus. Flirting. Fake flirting.

Owen took a seat opposite him at the two-person, white-clothed table.

"Uh, Owen?"

"Yes?"

"Daniel will never find me if you're camping here. Could you maybe wait at the bar for your parents? I can text you if you want to look busy."

"Thank you, no need. I'm not eating out with my parents tonight."

Jason frowned and looked around the room slowly. His heart had started a wild little throb in his chest, and all his limbs tingled. He wouldn't quite let himself get carried away on a stray thought, though. He swallowed hard. "Sister? Brother? Cop buddy? Former teacher?"

"No. No. No and no."

A waitress dropped off two glasses and a carafe of water.

Jason's gaze was suctioned onto Owen pouring them each a glass. Amusement played around the corners of his lips, his eyes. He looked so comfortable in his chair, his leather jacket slung over the back, his phone face down on the table. Like he was settling in to stay a while.

Owen flashed a hand for the waiter and asked politely if they'd light the candle.

A flame came to life between them. The waiter deposited their menus and left, and Jason stared at the gloss of light playing on that warm smile.

Owen leaned forward. "Get there quicker, sweetheart."

Earnest Point Police
@earnestpointcops

Barney, if we have to tell you one more time . . .

Chapter Eight

O
h God. No way. "Why didn't you tell me?"

The table felt smaller now, with all these jumbling emotions expanding inside Jason. Over the other side, Owen leaned back in his chair, an elbow tucked over its back. Effortless and at ease. "I wanted you to be as surprised as I have continuously been since meeting you. Disappointed?"

"But you . . . You're a cop, you shouldn't . . ."

"Be on Grindr? Have a sex life?"

"Have a fake identity?"

Owen just stared at him over the candelabra. And, yes, Jason saw the hypocrisy in that.

"I like to keep my private life discrete. Daniel's my middle name, I go by that online. Not that I'm on Grindr much. Barely at all, to be honest. A couple of times when I was trying to purge Hayden from my system."

Jason tried and failed to not picture Owen purging his system. His mind was on overdrive trying to fit him in a bed, glistening with sweat as he fucked a willing partner relentlessly into a mattress. All that raw strength and control and Owen . . . losing it at the end?

He shook his head. The table shrank further. The outline of Owen's legs blazed like a furnace under the table.

He fumbled for his water, catching the glass before it tipped over. "Not on there much? Except you were last night."

"I had some venting to do last night. With you."

"You . . . vented with me?"

Puzzlement and understanding, and the jerking of that heat near his legs. "No. This showing up here, this revealing of my identity to you, *that*'s me venting."

Jason laughed, grabbing at the sides of the menu. He was shaking. Partly a pleasant kind of ticklishness at the surprise, partly his brain working through the facts. There were just so many. Daniel was Owen. Which meant Jason had been messaging Owen last night from the next room. And *Owen* was the one willing to play the role of fake boyfriend. And Owen had known this wee fact all day. And Owen was definitely enjoying the look of shock on Jason's face.

And also: Owen was on Grindr. *Interested in LTR (long term relationship). Safe: PrEP, regular testing. Top.*

"So you don't usually use Grindr to hook up?"

Owen picked up his water and sipped, studying him thoughtfully. He set it down again. "I prefer the old-fashioned method of meeting in real life, and all the wonderful ways life can make that happen."

Jason tapped his fingers on the table, foot moving too. Bach, "Cello Suite No.1, Prelude".

After a moment, Owen asked, "You okay?"

Jason looked up into generous dark eyes. "Okay?"

"Good enough you won't get up and leave?"

"Why on earth would I do that? You're the most perfect man I could ever wish to be my fake boyfriend."

Teasingly, "Yet you never asked me to begin with."

Jason stopped tapping. "*That*'s the question you were expecting?"

"It didn't once cross your mind?"

"Of course it crossed my mind, and Cora's mind. I dismissed it immediately."

Wait staff came then to take their order, and Jason blindly chose the first thing his gaze latched onto.

Owen ordered more deliberately and turned his attention back to Jason. "Dismissed it?"

Jason wagged a finger at him. "Which I'll have to do again. It's all fine if my fake guy will never be seen or heard of in town again, but you . . . you're the pinnacle of everything wonderful around here. Everyone says as much."

Owen perked up at this. "Everyone?"

"When I ask, at work. And it's all over Twitter."

"You ask everyone about me?"

"*Subtly.*"

An eyebrow lifted. "What would *that* look like?"

Jason leaned forward on his chair. "Okay . . . for example, a plumber came in today and said Carl was probably due to have his gutters cleaned, a lot of leaks happened from blocked gutters in storms. So I said he should come around tomorrow, and he should do both our houses while he was at it, and he looked right at me and said Sergeant Stirling's? like he knew it was your house but might be wrong? Anyway, he murmured something about that being a neighbourly thing to do—which, side note, totally nailing the small-town attitude—and I replied that you'd helped me out a few times recently and it was the least I could do, and weren't we all lucky to have such a wonderful person keeping our town safe. See? Subtle. And he absolutely agreed. Best grin I saw all day. Well, until that one." Jason gestured to Owen's twinkly eyes and twitching mouth.

Jason continued, "This is all a roundabout way of saying you can't be my fake boyfriend. I'd ruin you."

Owen hummed to himself. "Quite possibly. I shouldn't . . ."

"You won't."

"I want to."

Dark eyes hit his, and Jason's heart sort of jumped. He wasn't used to such constant kindness. Sure, he had friendly neighbours back home, but none who he felt could be . . . friends. Carl was a fool for avoiding Owen like he had.

He reached out and laid a hand over Owen's. He was meant to insist that Owen shouldn't do this, that he'd find someone else. But fingers twitched under his and the words were robbed from him. "Owen," he whispered in a frantic effort not to give in, "I'd have to flirt with you in front of your friends. Alex."

Owen started to reply, but Jason needed him to understand. "That means PDA." He propped an elbow on the table, rested his chin in his hand, and looked past the flame at Owen swallowing down his response. "Little touches in public. Gazing at you with complete and utter adoration. It won't come naturally, so on top of putting up with it in public, you'd have to coach me in private."

"Coach you?" Disbelief.

"Exactly. See? Better I find someone else."

Owen flipped his hand under Jason's and the pocket of air between their palms thrummed, like his fingers did when he played—a magical stirring around his skin that slowly seeped into him, until it coursed head to toe. Fingers stroked over his palm. He shivered. "Yes, okay, I get it," Jason murmured. "It's not that you *couldn't* do an excellent job of coaching, it's just that . . . you know . . . how could I ever make it up you?"

"Jason, you—"

"Owen." The call came from close by, and Owen visibly froze at the sound of the man's voice. He didn't immediately turn to face the slender figure who approached with a taller, dapper-looking gentleman at his side.

Jason eyed the pair. They wore suits the same shade of grey and matching glasses, thickly rimmed, ruby. The smiles on their faces had a plastic feel to them, particularly the one who'd called Owen's name. Jason disliked *him* immediately—a gut response. The stiffness in Owen's shoulders as he faced them doubled his dislike. Owen drawing his fingers away cemented it.

"Hayden." Owen gave the taller one a cursory nod. "Kaden."

Jason almost giggled. Hayden and Kaden? In matching outfits? *Really?*

Wait—Hayden? As in Hayden who had left him on moving day? The man Owen had fallen in love with at first sight? The reason Owen no longer believed in that? Heartbreaker, soul crusher Hayden? Suddenly giggling seemed a very far off prospect.

Hayden gestured to the free table next to theirs. "Last one."

A glance around the restaurant proved that to be true. The remaining tables had filled up in the time Jason had been knocking knees with Owen.

Owen swallowed, Adam's apple jutting. "I see."

Hayden clapped a hand on Owen's upper arm and Jason's gaze narrowed to the squeeze pinching Owen's shirt. "You and Carl?" A barking laugh that didn't meet his eyes as he glanced at Jason. "I didn't think you were interested in him beyond his 'pretty face'. But all along, eh?"

Owen's expression was cool—years of police training no doubt coming into play—but the tautness of the air said everything. Jason felt for him.

Owen glanced toward the growing crowd of couples looking for a seat and gestured toward the free table. "Incoming. You might want to claim your spot."

Hayden hurried Kaden to their seats and fussed about with the table settings, while Jason tried to find a way to ask if Owen was okay without them overhearing. He caught Owen's restless gaze and steered a foot between his. A little nudge of their ankles, a jolt of electricity up Jason's calf—or maybe that was Owen's slightly surprised shift—before he answered Jason's question by nudging back.

Jason wanted to go back to the way it had been only moments before. Owen's genuine ease and all those little grins twitching at his mouth.

Hayden conversed with Kaden like he wanted everyone to know how lucky he was. *You're incredible, Kaden. . . . Gosh, so smart, Kaden. . . . I love how talented you are, Kaden.*

Owen kept his attention on Jason, but how he managed with all that . . . Jason was affronted on his behalf at the lack of tact. If Caroline had done that, he'd have been wishing the ground would suck him up whole.

"Excuse me," Owen said, rising from his chair. "Men's room."

Jason hoped the cop would have a moment to punch a wall.

As soon as Owen was out of sight, Hayden waved a hand. Jason thought about ignoring it, but decided he wouldn't play games. He'd act as maturely as he could in front of Owen's ex.

"Carl, looking forward to Pete and Nick's stag night? Those boys know how to have fun, hm?"

Why was he bringing Pete up like this? "Sure do."

"It'll be tough writing up toasts for their long happy marriage, though, won't it?"

Was he trying to pick at wounds? "I'll be fine."

Hayden's lip curled. Not getting the response he was after, was he?

"Do they have a musician for the wedding yet?"

"I'm not sure."

Hayden gestured to Kaden. "I got lucky with this one." The emphasis on *this* felt pointed. And, frankly, mean.

A waiter approached with Jason and Owen's food, and

Hayden stopped him along the way. "We made a request to play three pieces on the piano. Is now good?"

They got the go ahead, and in the time it took Jason to have his own quiet word with the waiter, Hayden had Kaden seated at the grand piano and was back in his seat.

He leaned toward Jason, eyes on the plates being trucked back to the kitchens. "Something not to your liking?"

"Something," Jason said.

Music caught Jason's attention; he listened courteously, as he would to any musician—Mozart's "Sonata No. 16, Sonata Facile". A great piece for beginner to intermediate players.

He applauded along with most of the room, and caught Hayden noting Owen's return. Hayden lifted his voice. "Isn't he wonderful?"

Jason ground his teeth against the urge to snap. How dare he flaunt what he considered 'better' in front of Owen. "That sonata was a good choice for his skill level. No breakneck semi-quavers to contend with."

Hayden shifted his attention to Jason, narrowing his eyes. "It was incredible. Better than either of us could do."

Jason itched to stand, ask Kaden if he wouldn't mind shuffling over, and play Chopin's "Fantasie-Impromptu". Put this jerk in his place.

He gripped the seat of his chair. *Carl* wouldn't know Chopin's "Fantasie-Impromptu". In fact, judging by the state of Carl's piano, he'd be lucky if he knew "Three Blind Mice". And Kaden was not the problem here. He shouldn't be made collateral damage.

Hayden shifted his chair back from where he'd inched it during Kaden's performance and looked up, tracking Owen's progress through the maze of tables. "Bit of a rebound thing, hmm? After Pete?"

It was all said with smiles. And with the underlying assumption Owen would only be an interim measure. Like he'd once been for Hayden.

And Jason. Did. Not. Like it.

Before Owen could drop into his seat, Jason stood, a ticklish, protective fury sweeping through him. He moved closer to Owen, so tall and beautiful in his pressed shirt, and picked up his leather jacket.

Owen's eyes shifted from Jason to Hayden to Kaden playing "Ode to Joy". He raised a questioning brow.

"Our food is being packed."

"I can make it through dinner," Owen said quietly.

Jason met his eyes. "You, maybe. I can't." He opened the leather jacket and Owen slipped an arm inside, letting Jason steer the rest onto his broad shoulders.

Owen growled, stormy eyes sliding to Hayden. "Did he say something?"

Jason straightened the leather, hands gripping the jacket at Owen's chest. "Not exactly, but I'm about to." He yanked Owen closer and this time Owen folded into the small space between them, all undulating muscle, bergamot and lavender, and puffed breath over Jason's nose. "You're the most amazing guy I have ever met. I want to meet your parents and thank them for raising someone so kind and heroic." Easy to catch his eye and pronounce this. It was *true*. "I still don't know how I can ever do enough for you, but if you give me a chance, I want . . ." His voice broke then, and heat flooded his face. Fake boyfriends. He wanted to do this with Owen. "I want . . ."

Jason had started this aware of Hayden watching them, listening; aware of the music clattering out from the stage; but somewhere along the way, he'd become aware of *himself*. How close he stood to Owen, how warm his limbs were, how his fingers trembled against the leather.

A stray lash balanced on the crest of Owen's cheek, candlelight reflected in those dark eyes. Light hands had settled on his hips and slid to the small of his back.

Owen dipped a smiling face and spoke in his ear. "What do you want?"

Hands tightened warmly around him and Jason flowed with it, drunk on bergamot and a shared smile. Sergeant Owen Daniel Stirling Sir had a killer smile. And his heavy voice spilled from between them, almost tangible. His breath had a dense quality to it too, powerful. Ploughing through the middle of his own, which came out shallow, hectic. A little like his heart, ramming about in his chest.

A broken whisper, "To be yours."

A flash of something hit Owen's eyes and—

Applause filled the room.

He jerked back, sinking onto his heels, and Owen loosened his hold, a whoosh of cardamom-spiced air taking up the space between them.

Kaden had finished playing. Right.

Oh, and Hayden was staring at them. Just as, ah, Jason had intended. He rocked on his feet again, grinned at Owen, and jerked his thumb toward the door. "Shall we get out of here?"

Earnest Point Police
@earnestpointcops

A storm's coming in, folks. You know the drill. Stay at home when you can. Stay under the speed limit when you can't. To those dudes who reckon they are so cool and invincible, maybe don't try to prove it on the highway today.

Chapter Nine

A thirty-second car ride brought them to another beach; a sand-sunken bench glimmered in the setting sun, and the way Owen ran his fingers over it suggested he knew the spot well.

They set up a makeshift picnic and took turns poking at one another's dinner with wooden forks. Owen's was the best.

Jason turned toward him and propped his elbow on the back of the bench, the last of the food between them. "I'm not the biggest seafood fan."

"From the man who ordered mussels."

"I was distracted." Gently, Jason prodded Owen's nose with the end of his fork. "You were very distracting."

A laugh, low and rumbly like the waves crashing against the shore. That frame of his, relaxed, casual, yet ready to coil and spring into action in a moment. Jason wanted all that, craved that poise, that fairness. Also firmness. So much firmness. What would it take to have that, embody that?

"*Were?*"

Jason dragged his gaze from the buttons of Owen's stretched shirt to crinkled eyes. "Hmm?"

Owen speared a last mussel, then looked at Jason thoughtfully. "I thought you were determined to find someone else?"

Jason had been expecting that question, of course. He flushed at the quiet rumble of it. "Hayden changed my mind."

A perplexed frown.

"What did you ever see in him!"

Owen raised a brow and, okay, Jason should calm it down. "What did you, ah, ever see in him?"

Owen laughed, then sighed, gazing at the last of the gold sinking toward the horizon. A blaze of pinks and purples reflected off all that blond hair. "I suppose I find high energy and spontaneity attractive."

"Until he spontaneously decides to be an"—a look from Owen, and Jason once again lowered his voice—"arse."

"He likes being the centre of attention, being special. And showing off his boyfriends, as it turns out. I was fun for a while, but the fun wore out."

That protective fury fizzed in Jason's veins again. "Impossible."

"Is that right?"

"I'm even more convinced we need to be boyfriends."

Sunset glowed over Owen's smile.

"He'll be at the stag night and the wedding, and I'm going to be spontaneous all over you until he's seething with jealousy."

Owen was suddenly standing up, hammering a fist to his chest, making some kind of choking sound; Jason was on his feet in the sand, rubbing his back. His circles got wider, slower. "You okay?"

"No. No, I'm not." But he was . . . laughing now? Sighing?

Jason steadied himself, arms wrapping around that broad chest. "You choked like that on your coffee this morning. You might need to get that looked at."

"I know what the problem is. I'm fine. I'll be fine. I hope."

Owen glanced over his shoulder, recovered now thank God, and . . . this was . . . comfortable. Too comfortable to move. So Jason grinned and settled his chin on Owen's shoulder. "Owen, I'd like you to be my fake boyfriend, but if you change your mind at any point—"

"Thank you. I'm good for now."

Jason let out a relieved breath. "I promise, when we stage the breakup I'll be the one at fault. You'll come away looking like such a saint, all the gay boys will be after you." He squeezed Owen reassuringly. "In the meantime, could we practice, you know, being together?"

OWEN SHOOK HIS HEAD IN DISBELIEF THE ENTIRE WAY HOME. Jason felt similarly. It was . . . surreal. Once again, by indulging him in this charade, Owen was coming to Jason's rescue. But . . . it was kind of exciting too? His body vibrated with the adventure of it all, starting off in low ticklish tones and climbing higher and higher. Grieg, "In the Hall of the Mountain King".

This time when Jason followed Owen into his house, step bouncing, Owen didn't even look surprised. He just found a clean toothbrush and a towel and handed them over with another shake of his head. "No snakes will hurt you."

"Especially not in your bed."

"Oh, good lord. Guest room."

"But Mary isn't here."

An exasperated look.

Jason followed Owen down the hall towards the bedrooms. "We need to talk about dinner with my family tomorrow night. We should hold it here, obviously."

"Obviously?"

"I know your kitchen better than Carl's."

Owen flung a door open. "In you go."

Jason backed in reluctantly. "Also, I don't expect you to get your parents involved. That would be asking too much, even if I'm kinda curious who raised you. But we can say something came up last minute. A cold maybe."

"To be honest, Jason, after tonight my parents probably already know——" A phone buzzed from Owen's pocket and he fished it out. "Speak of the devil . . . Mum. Yes——Of course. Tomorrow, my place. Say,"——he looked over at Jason, resigned and finding the humour in it all——"six?"

Jason gave him double thumbs up, but his stomach took a wee dive to his groin. Oh God, he was going to meet parents. The last time he'd done that had been with Caroline's and that had been awkward at best. Sure, this was fake, but his curiosity wasn't, and none of his enjoyment of the evening would be either.

He'd have to make something spectacular. A wee bit exotic. Something that would leave an impression. Both families would have questions, of course, and he and Owen should be prepared to answer them all.

Owen laughed and said, "You don't need to bring anything——"

Within the second, Jason had the phone out of Owen's hand and pressed to his ear. "Hello, the secret boyfriend here. Yes, Carl. That's me. Mrs Stirling—— . . . Renee, of course. There *is* something you could bring . . ."

Two minutes later, Jason ended the call, chuckling. "Nice parents."

Owen had taken a post against the doorframe, arms folded, to watch Jason talk. Now he pushed off the wall, took his phone from Jason's hand and tucked it into a back pocket. "My photo album?"

Jason felt that stare in his stomach, which . . . was still lodged in his groin. And, um, it didn't have to move anytime soon. "I had to establish credibility. I'm head over heels for you, remember?"

～

SOMEHOW, HE MADE IT THROUGH THE NIGHT WITHOUT BOLTING out of the guest bed and into Owen's. Having him just one wall over helped, but not nearly enough for a good night's rest.

Once they were up, though, the time flew by; they were soon driving into town, listening to the weather channel. It looked okay outside now, splotches of blue in the sky at least, but around midnight a cyclone was expected to whip through.

"Hold it," Jason said, slapping a hand to Owen's T-shirt sleeve. "Why aren't you in uniform? Is it casual day at the station?"

"No casual day." Owen navigated an intersection. "I'm not on shift today."

"What?"

"We work on a revolving roster. I have today off."

Jason glanced at the dashboard clock. "Why aren't you sleeping in?"

"Alex still has your Jeep."

"It's . . . not raining. I could've walked."

Owen side-eyed him. "*This* is something I would do for my boyfriend."

Jason fuzzed with warmth, and he had a sudden need to retie a loose shoelace. He did so, chuckling. "How on earth are you still single?"

When he looked over, Owen was tapping a silent beat on the steering wheel, smiling out into the distance.

Jason's phone buzzed. A reminder. "Guttering starts at nine this morning."

"Thank you for taking care of that. Gives me time to shop for our dinner."

"I know. Big list. I just . . . want tonight to be perfect? The last time I met parents . . ."

"The last time, what?" Owen asked.

Jason flushed and gave him a fleeting glance. "Nothing terrible, just they didn't think I was good enough. It was kind of hard to shake."

"You know it doesn't matter what my parents think, right?"

"It's all fake, sure, but—"

"That's not what I meant." Owen stopped the car just outside the convenience store, engine running. "Jason, look at me."

Owen rested one hand on the wheel, the other on his thigh, and fixed dark eyes on Jason's. "What my parents—what anyone—thought of my boyfriend wouldn't matter. If I reckon he's good enough, that's all that matters. And Jason?"

"Owen?"

"As my boyfriend, you're frighteningly wonderful."

Frighteningly wonderful. "I wish the frightening part would go away."

"Believe me, so do I."

Jason tossed him a grin. He sure had caught them both up in a web of lies. Whatever happened, he would not let Owen be hurt by them. He would absolutely play the bad guy when it came time to break up. And he'd make sure to frame Owen as the most desirable gay man in Tasmania.

Although, to be fair, he was pretty much there already. Calendar Cop looks, protective, strong, decent . . . would even shop for hard-to-come-by, quite expensive ingredients on his day off. Oh—"Do you want to take my card?"

Groaning, "God, yes."

Jason fished it out of his wallet, and Owen pushed it all back to him. "Out of the car, sweetheart."

A sigh. "I wish I didn't have to work. I'd much rather spend the day with you."

"What about all our town folk with donut needs?"

"Fine. I'll spend the day inside creaming my pants instead."

Owen leaned over, air waking over Jason with a shiver, and opened his door.

Jason reluctantly hopped out and ducked his head back inside. "Pick me up early?"

"Sure."

Jason winked. "Then thinking cap on, cupid—we need a meet cute. And some practice at public affection."

JASON DROPPED THE HOROSCOPES HE'D BEEN READING AND rounded the counter, batting his loose flannel out of the way, as Pete stumbled into the store near closing time. "Mate, what happened?"

Pete lifted warm, tired eyes and threw his arms around Jason's chest. He looked wrecked. Ginger hair in all directions, bags under his eyes. "I haven't slept in days. Poor Nick came down with something and it hasn't cleared up yet. I need to take care of him. We'll have to shift the stag night."

Jason bit down on a *Thank Fuck*. He frowned sympathetically. "What about Angus?" Whoever Angus was.

"Ha! Angus will have to wait."

"Disappointing."

"Tell me about it." From his back pocket he pulled out a folded piece of paper. "So. Bit of a pickle. Our pick for the music fell through."

Jason took the paper and read over Nick's wish list. All classical pieces. All familiar.

"Would you mind calling around the schools and seeing if you can find a group who could play any of these? At this point, I'd even settle for bagpipes, as long as there's some music for the reception. I hope Owen isn't stealing all your time."

He knew about Owen? Some grapevine.

He probably ought to call his brother about this teeny tiny development.

"I must admit, it took some getting my head around. I thought you didn't get on?"

Jason opened his mouth and shut it again. "People change. I've changed."

"I did a number on you, didn't I?" he said quietly. "That's why you're rebounding with him."

Jason moved abruptly back around the counter. The second time someone had assumed Owen could only be a temporary fix. The man deserved better. "I never gave Owen the chance he deserved before. I wish I had. He's so goddamn perfect."

An older patron cleared his throat and came smiling up to the counter. His vest had the same grey and blue pattern as his tartan cap and there was something about his dark eyes that had Jason staring. The way those spectacles magnified the twinkle in them, probably. "The donuts for now, thanks."

He shuffled out of the store, and Pete draped himself over the counter. He caught sight of the horoscopes and twisted the magazine toward himself. A jovial snicker. "You and those things. What's mine? I've found the love of my life and will live happily ever after?"

Tough to hear, if he were Carl. Thank God Jason was here to smile gaily and read out Pete's horoscope, which promised a lover's spat and had Pete grabbing the honey he'd come for and racing off home.

A bark came from outside.

The doors slid open and Alex and Mary raced in. Or more accurately, Mary raced in towing Alex behind her.

Jason went to his knees to welcome her back, cooing about how much he'd missed her last night, as Alex handed him the lead.

"Would you mind looking after her until Uncle Owen gets back? I tried calling him but it went straight to voicemail and I have a . . . study session tonight." Alex brightened, and Jason couldn't help grinning.

"How much studying will there be?"

"Lots."

Mary barked, and Alex and Jason sighed in unison. "No worries. Have fun, Alex. Don't drive in the storm."

He nodded and raced off, and Jason rubbed behind Mary's floppy ears. "Now look here, Mary Puppins, none of that tonight. I need you on your best, most lenient behaviour. A few falsehoods might pop up here and there, but you have to understand, Owen and I are both aware of what's true and what's not."

She licked his face.

He laughed and patted her again. "Want to check out the doggie aisle? Come on."

∾

OWEN FOUND JASON CRAWLING OUT OF A DOGHOUSE. JASON gulped and slowly looked up those dark jeans to darker eyes filled with bewilderment.

Mary sat regal and elegant at his side, like she had nothing to do with this. Traitor.

"It's not what it looks like?"

"It looks like you're emerging from a doghouse."

"Okay, so it *is* what it looks like, but—"

"Are you wearing a collar?"

The leather was far too warm around his neck. "Yes, but only because I'm pretending to be a dog!"

Silence.

Jason sat back on his haunches. "Mary kept jumping on top

of the houses, and I was just trying to show her how to use them properly."

"I'm curious at what point you decided a collar was the way to go."

"She still didn't get it after I crawled in and out the first time, so I thought if I looked the part and barked around a bit . . . can we pretend this never happened?"

Jason held a hand up and Owen pulled him to his feet, expression unfathomable.

Jason felt for the buckle at his throat. "Thank God only you and that one other man saw me."

"Someone else saw you?"

"An older guy came in a few times—he saw me trying to push Mary inside one time. Actually, *he* was the one who suggested I act it out for her."

Owen's brow crunched and he rubbed at the creases. "This man. He didn't happen to have spectacles, did he? Wear a cap?"

"Loves tartan."

"That rascal."

"You know him?"

"Like the back of my hand. That, Jason, was my dad. Nathan."

Jason groaned, dropping his head. Had he come in to spy on his son's secret boyfriend? "I wanted to make a good first impression, not—"

Gently, Owen raised Jason's chin. A soft smile. "You definitely made his day. Probably his week, maybe even the entire month." Fingers fluttered under his jaw and down his neck to the collar. A hum of laughter buzzed at his cheek. "Mine, too."

Jason's breath came out light and uneven.

Carefully, Owen plucked at the buckle, and the collar loosened. A finger wriggled under the strap, over the point where

Jason's pulse pounded. It lingered there a few seconds, then the leather came off his neck in a long, shivery slide.

Jason extracted himself from the thin air between them.

He was . . . all nerves, his whole body thrumming with anticipation. They would have to act . . . close. *Like lovers . . .*

There was so much to get right. Their parents would be analysing everything. Including these mortifying sneak peeks of him before dinner had even started, apparently. Not exactly the most dignified beginning.

He rolled his shoulders and locked up shop.

Never mind. It wasn't like things could get worse.

"OH GOD, OH *GOD*. I'VE KILLED HER."

Jason paced outside the ER, away from a distraught Cora in the waiting room. They hadn't even made it to dinner. The second Jason and Owen had arrived home, they'd been pounced upon by their families, who were all too eager to wait for six o'clock. Which meant there'd been no time to practice anything or come up with their story, and in a fit of nerves, Jason had beelined Owen into the kitchen to help make cocktails.

A nice way for everyone to relax.

Or so he'd thought.

He tipped his head toward the dark sky. Wind was really whipping around them now. Rain dropped into his eyes. "Oh God."

Owen latched onto his hand and pulled him close, tucking him against his chest. "She's fine. She had her epi pen, and she's being checked for good measure. You haven't killed anyone."

Jason wriggled closer and ground his forehead on Owen's shoulder. "*Pineapple.*"

A soft sigh breezed warmly through his hair.

"Carl never would have . . ."

"You're not Carl."

"Please, please don't tell her I did it. I mean, of course you have to tell her, but I really don't want her to know."

Owen shifted them, shielding Jason from the thickening rain. "This was an accident. Deep breaths. In . . . and out. . . . And in."

Jason breathed deeply, the air cocooned between them a soft, living thing. It expanded through him with medicinal calm, and slowly, slowly he stopped shaking. Hands kept stroking him. They'd both left their jackets at home in the rush, and Owen's warm palms made an imaginary blanket over his back.

"Thank you, Owen."

"For what?"

"Not throwing me in jail for negligent almost-manslaughter?"

"It wasn't even close. You got that pen in her within seconds, Jason. I've never seen you move so fast, and boy have I seen you move fast."

Jason laughed and squeezed Owen's sides with his wrists, hands balled in T-shirt. "Don't make me laugh. I'm drowning in remorse."

"How about doing that another time, hm? Patricia and Cora are coming out and they look just fine."

Jason snapped his head up. There they were, aunt and niece, arm in arm and heading towards them.

Jason let go of Owen and darted over, fuelled on the energy of guilt and relief. Patricia looked a little flushed, but she was breathing.

"How are you?"

"What was that?" she called over a whistling wind.

"How are you?"

She nodded. "Fine, darling. The wind. Let's chat in the car."

Chat.

Oh, Christ. He had to tell them what happened. Jason's stomach knotted and the car came into view far too quickly for his liking.

Jason slung himself in the front beside Owen and they were all belted in and sealed off from the howling wind within the minute. When he twisted to look Patricia—healthy, smiling even—over, Cora was patting her arm across the middle seat. Side by side, the resemblance between them was striking— Cora could have been the Patricia of twenty years ago.

She murmured jokingly, "Your horoscope did say there'd be some ups and downs this month . . ."

"Sorry, Mum," Jason said quietly. They both looked at him, then Cora quickly looked out the window. "I was nervous, about tonight—I thought cocktails would help—"

"And I completely forgot about your allergy, Patricia," Owen said smoothly, turning out onto the road.

Jason startled.

"It's okay. You don't have to take the blame for me, Carl. You told me about the allergy and I forgot." He looked in the rear-view mirror. "I hope you'll forgive me."

Patricia waved a hand. "Let's just call this memorable."

Jason would remember it all right. This swooping relief, and this tender fluttering in his chest. Owen, cop, upholder of the law, lying on his behalf. Taking this weight from him.

He rubbed his chest over the throb.

"Speaking of," Patricia continued, gesturing between them, "you've been neighbours for years. How did this happen?"

Oh *God*! They'd had no time—

Owen landed a hand on Jason's thigh and squeezed, flooding him with silent assurances. *Nothing to worry about.* A gentle rub followed another squeeze and Owen's laugh turned into a story. A . . . familiar one. "There was an issue one night with a wallaby."

"Would we call it a wallaby? Not a crazed kangaroo?"

Owen's lips curled. "Crazed, all right. I came over to help him out, and something just clicked between us. It was like . . . I'd never really seen him before."

Their eyes met, and Jason smirked quietly. "Exactly the same for me. You were like this glorious god on my porch, absolutely glistening with—" He sat straighter in his seat. Probably not the details to give 'Mum'. "I mean, uh, you were very kind, and within a few days I knew you were a man I needed in my life." He looked back at Patricia and a very curious Cora. "In fact, I've practically been living with him since. And now here we are, sharing this with you."

A gust of wind rocked the car. A deafening rumble. Owen braked, flinging out an arm against Jason's chest. Violent rain drove against the roof, the road. Through it, Jason glimpsed soil and half a tree that had slipped to the road. Owen eyed the banks and trees to their left. "Right."

He threw an arm behind Jason's seat and reversed deftly until he reached a turning bay. He drove swiftly out of the hilly range and pulled over under the cover of a gas station to make a call. "Mum? The road to my place is blocked from the cyclone. Prepare the spare beds, Jason and I are staying with you and bringing Cora and Patricia with us." A throaty laugh, and a look at Jason. "It was quite the night."

Jason smiled sheepishly as Owen put the car in gear and drove back out into the storm. He had rather complicated this whole twin-swap, hadn't he? He should be careful not to get carried away again.

"Oh God, stop the car!"

Owen came to a controlled stop. "You all right?"

Jason stared out through the slanting rain. He made out the form of a cat lying on the side of the road, under a tree. Could it still be alive? Ten years ago, his own precious Casper had been lost like that. He'd been devastated. He'd always thought, if someone had spotted him early enough . . .

He twisted to Cora. "That blanket behind you—pass it to me?"

She did.

He clicked open his belt and Owen planted a staying hand on his shoulder. "What are you doing?"

"Phone an after-hours vet." He jumped out of the car into a beasty wind. Rain sluiced over his face and down his neck, but he was across the road in seconds. Leaves from a fallen branch partially obscured the cat. It wasn't . . . it wasn't moving. But it was still warm. He thought he felt a heartbeat.

A car door shut.

He used the blanket to scoop the poor thing up, covering it to keep it from going into shock.

Footsteps splashed toward him and Owen was at his side, holding another blanket up over them. It was cop Owen. Concerned and capable. "Got it?"

Jason nodded and they hurried back into the car. He cradled the poor thing and peeked under the blankets, but in the dark it was hard to see. No blood as far as he could make out. Funny-looking though. A breed he wasn't familiar with. Bit of a long snout, wasn't it?

Um, too long?

Those claws . . .

Oh, God.

It twitched on his lap, and he froze in his seat.

Had he, er, seen one of these once? At the zoo?

Patricia and Cora were chatting in the backseat, and Jason whispered, "Owen?"

"Hm?"

"You know how you said this has been quite the night . . ."

Owen glanced at him and did a double-take, probably at

the fear crystalised on Jason's face. His gaze dropped to the blankets and up again, and it was like . . . he knew. He could read every one of Jason's freaked-out spasms.

Jason lifted a shaky finger to his lips and nodded as smoothly as he could toward the audience in the backseat. Probably . . . probably a local would have recognised this cat for what it really was. Carl would never have made this mistake.

Owen gassed it up a cul-de-sac and as he drove up a long gravel driveway, he reached over and tugged down the blanket with a dry "What the devil" and a disbelieving headshake.

Jason squeaked out a laugh. "Just a wee oopsie."

From the back, Cora leaned forward. "Oopsie?"

Widened eyes. "The uh, cat scratched me a little. Nothing to worry about."

Owen parked. "Cora, Patricia, go on in, my parents are expecting you. We'll just get our . . . cat to safety."

As soon as their doors shut, Owen was once again reversing. Speedily.

"Will the vet be able to help it?"

"I'd say it's just gone into torpor."

"Sounds serious."

A groaning laugh. "Torpor means it's playing dead."

The devil in his lap twitched.

His heart jumped into his throat. "These devils are kind, cuddly creatures, aren't they? Badly named, that's all. That cartoon one was all exaggerated. Right?" Another stirring on his lap. "Pleasedon'tsayotherwise."

"Won't say otherwise," Owen said, pulling over and swiftly getting out of the car.

"That says otherwise!" His exclamation came out a whisper as the bundle started wriggling.

Owen quietly opened Jason's door and rapidly slipped his hands around the blanketed devil. Suddenly there was a frenzy of movement and pressure at his terrified crotch, and Jason was of two minds about it. The bigger mind wanted it over, all wriggling to cease, pronto. The smaller mind was quite taken with how calmly Owen was handling it all. Each shift of his hands danced over sensitive spaces, protecting them from rather pointy claws. Something snagged on his inner thigh.

A blood-curdling demonic shriek filled the car.

It wasn't coming from the Tasmanian Devil.

Jason could see the appeal of "torpor", or whatever. *I'm nothing interesting. Take those claws and let me be.*

Owen got the devil in a firm hold and raced him into the nearby bush. Other cries emanated from the wilderness, and then Owen came charging back through the rain, laughing.

Behind the wheel, he looked at Jason in amused exasperation.

"I know," Jason rubbed his face. "I'm a magnet for misadventure."

"A *magnificent* magnet for misadventure."

Yeah.

Owen palmed Jason's thigh, dragging his index finger along the inner seam. What had just been terrorised was suddenly tingling. "Did it get you?"

Jason blinked, startled, and looked down. Owen was outlining a small tear in his jeans.

Oh. He squeezed his thighs together and shook his head. "Ah, I'm fine. Just got the denim."

"Thank you."

"Oh yes, thank you, Sergeant Owen Stirling. Sir."

"That wasn't a directive, Jason." Jason lifted his gaze from the large, dexterous hand trapped between his suddenly frozen thighs. "Thank you for picking up the devil. Not many would help a marsupial stuck on the road during a cyclone."

"I'm not sure I deserve praise for a case of mistaken identity."

"Hmm. I'm definitely thankful despite"—Owen met his eyes—"mistaken identity. And I feel . . ."

"What?"

"Even if you thought you only loved cats and would only ever stop for a cat, actually you're discovering you would stop for other things. And they might become tolerable to you. Special, even."

"Oh, Owen. I know exactly what you're saying."

Owen let out a long breath, ticklishly dragged his fingers free, and started the car.

"But I have to say, it'd have to be some snake for me to find it special."

OWEN'S PARENTS' HOUSE WAS BROWN STONE WITH WHITE TRIM, two-storey—warm light was spilling from a large bay window, an inviting beacon in a storm. Blanket covering their heads, Owen raced him up to the porch, where his mum and dad— and Mary, who they'd offered to take during the hospital rush —were waiting for them. Matching tartan dressing gowns enfolded them in hugs and shut the door on the wailing of the storm.

"Good of you to take care of that cat." A pat on Jason's shoulder. Jason looked up into Nathan's crinkled eyes. "Just like my Owen. Such a good heart. He picked an injured devil up off the road once; helped it even though it scratched him up in the process."

Jason shook his head at Owen. "He left out that little story."

"Oh," Renee said. "I'm sure there are many stories he's 'left out'." She clapped her hands, and Owen's eyes widened.

Jason tucked a laughing face behind Owen and followed him and his family into the living room. Mary ambled straight over to a sheepskin near one of the two lamps that gently lit the cosy space, circled three times, and flopped down with a soft huff.

Patricia and Cora, it seemed, had gone straight to their beds, and with Renee and Nathan lounging against a mass of cushions on the couch—no tartan in here, just soft reds and golds—Owen had settled into the armchair.

Jason trucked up and down the living area, partly to satisfy his curiosity about where Owen had grown up, and partly because he wasn't sure if he should sit at Owen's feet or sling himself onto his lap. He hoped the lack of 'practice' between them wasn't starting to show.

The room was filled with knickknacks and little collections of sculpted fruit in terracotta, porcelain, wood. They spoke of travels and interests and a voracious . . . love of stone fruit?

Jason's gaze wandered over wax-dribbled candles, an old pin cushion, a wooden bird feeder with the words *Love from Owen* burned into the side.

He grinned and carried on, absorbing all the clues, until a candid family picture caught his eye. Parents and two young children, a boy and a girl. They were laughing, playing chase at the beach . . . a familiar backdrop. He recognised the rock formation, the way the shore curved.

This was the spot Owen had taken him to. Twice.

A place he and his family cherished?

A special spot?

Owen's mother's voice startled him out of the touching thought. "Oh damn, sorry Carl—we left the photo album at Owen's place."

When he'd requested they bring along the family album, it'd seemed the perfect boyfriend thing to do. Pity pineapple had gone and ruined his chance to look at it. He'd been looking forward to seeing toddler Owen. It was . . . quite hard to imagine all that dazzling togetherness had ever thrown a tantrum.

Of course there was always tomorrow, but alone, without parental fondness wrapping the little images with affection and humour . . .

Not the same.

"Wait, I have some in the kitchen china cabinet." Music. To. His. Ears.

"What? Which?" Owen asked, alarmed.

"Those ones you keep trying to throw out."

Owen stirred in his chair, hand tapping restlessly on his knee. "You saved them *again?*"

"You can't toss out memories like that, son."

The flush on Owen's cheeks. Colour Jason intrigued. "What are these memories, Owen?"

"Nothing you need to see."

"He was about thirteen, maybe fourteen," Renee said. "He thought he looked like a wrestler, but really he was a gangly teenager in his grandma's skimpy leotards that she hadn't worn since the eighties. Lots of spandex."

Jason sank to his knees between Owen's legs and clasped his hands together. His forearms butted denim-clad inner thighs that squeezed against him briefly in surprise. "Please?"

Renee and Nathan erupted into yawns and stretches and suddenly they were heading to bed, their slippered steps sloughing down the hall.

Owen closed his eyes briefly. "Bed is an excellent idea."

"But you . . . in leotards."

Owen hauled him to his feet and marched him away from the kitchen and its china cabinet.

Laughter bubbled out of him. "I'll get my hands on those pictures, Sergeant Owen Stirling, Sir."

A curled whisper at his nape. "Just you try."

Jason rubbed the ticklish spot. *Challenge accepted.* He'd sneak out of the guestroom as soon as Owen's back was turned—

Owen flung open a door. Struck the light.

The moment he saw the Socceroos poster pinned above the king-single bed, it hit him: there'd be no sneaking out of the *guestroom.*

Gravity fled and his stomach dove after it. He spun around. "I get to sleep with you?"

Earnest Point Police
@earnestpointcops

It's cold out folks, but that doesn't
mean you have to be cold-
hearted. Look after each other.

Chapter Ten

Owen cupped his hips with cop-like efficiency and steered Jason into his childhood bedroom, over a wool rug, past a net of soccer and basket balls, to a blanketed trunk near a sturdy desk. Was this where young Owen had written his essays? Studied for his exams? A few stacks of books sat at one end. *Mysteries.* Hard boiled cops and cozies. He knew it!

Jason's arse hit the trunk. Owen told him to stay put and kept one eye on him as he fished for T-shirts from his drawers. He passed one over. "For bed."

Jason fingered the soft material as he eyed the king single. Owen was measuring it too. It was suddenly hard to imagine them both fitting in there. In fact, it was hard to imagine just Owen fitting in there.

A tiny nervous thrill zig-zagged through him. Well, anyone popping their head in tomorrow morning would believe they were boyfriends.

Jason gulped and jerked his attention to the rug. "Is this where all the leotard action happened?"

Owen laughed, then turned away from Jason and the shirt

he was practically inhaling. "Get changed and make yourself at home."

"Where are you going?"

"To shower." Quieter. "Or I'll get dirty all over you."

"You smell good to me."

The door shut with a decided snick.

Jason stripped and pulled Owen's large T-shirt over his head, but he didn't climb into bed. This was his chance, and he fully intended to take it—find these photos, bring one back and plant it on the pillow, then peek out between his lashes to watch Owen's reaction.

Maybe Jason would have to jump onto his back so he couldn't reach the bin to throw it away. Or maybe Owen would scoop him up and drop him on the living room couch as punishment—he'd still have Mary, so he could live with that.

He couldn't really say why he was so insistent on playing this game, but . . . it felt teasing, light-hearted, very much what a boyfriend might do for fun.

Dressed in nothing but his boxers and Owen's T-shirt, Jason snuck into the dark hall. Strips of light came from a bathroom halfway up, just before the stairs. He tiptoed along. The last thing he needed was Owen recognising the groan of wood.

He didn't make it to the stairs.

He was blocked by a tartan dressing gown and an old man with a mischievous grin. "You all right there, Carl?"

Jason's gaze darted around for an explanation. He couldn't very well say he wanted to sneak about in the kitchen. It wasn't particularly dignified behaviour for a guest in their home, and quite frankly, Owen's dad had seen him behave peculiarly enough today.

"Just, um, I was . . ." He jerked his thumb towards the bathroom door and the sound of rushing water coming from the shower behind it.

"I see." Nathan gestured down the narrow hallway toward the door, a sort of *you first*.

Jason's pulse picked up a few paces. "Oh." He floundered. "I guess I'll wait—it'll be locked."

"Nonsense. None of these old locks have their keys anymore."

Right.

His scalp prickled with sweat.

So. This was happening.

He moved to the bathroom door and slunk quietly through it, his back towards the interior. He shut the door and a towel fell off the back of it. Over the gushing water behind him he could hear a high humming. Rebecca Clarke's "Piano Trio"?

He forced himself not to whirl around in surprise. It was a well-known piece. Anyone might hum it without even realising what it was, except . . .

Never mind that. The door. He'd focus on that for the time it took Nathan to move on down the hallway, then he'd sneak out as softly as he came in and dive into Owen's bed. Enough adventure for tonight. Leotards would have to wait.

The sounds of Owen showering behind him were like a waterfall of shivers down his back. He pressed one ear against the door, hoping he might hear if the hallway was clear. Useless. He sank onto his knees on the soft towel and peered through the old keyhole.

A flash of movement.

Floorboards creaking, and the pad of paws. A voice, Renee's this time, urging Mary to follow.

But Mary—that was the flash of movement he'd seen—was approaching the bathroom. Great. How long would he be trapped in here—

A rumble of plastic on runners.

Gosh. It'd gone awfully quiet . . .

"Christ!"

Jason froze as steam and Owen's shock flooded over him, hot and moist on his bare legs and nape.

This was . . . not ideal.

Renee was close, possibly within earshot. It wouldn't make sense for Jason's 'boyfriend' to be too shocked by his being in here. In fact, a boyfriend might enjoy being joined in the shower.

On the other hand, this whole thing was fake and Owen might not appreciate this level of intrusion into his privacy. Jason's palms grew clammy where they were pressed—along with his face—against the door. How to handle this?

In his panic, voice husky with nerves, he blurted, "Mmm, nice surprise I hope?"

Short silence and stirring air. "Definitely a surprise. Can I?"

A naked foot landed by his knee, and Jason caught a glimpse of a wet leg. A wall of heat buffered up close behind him and Jason didn't understand what Owen was doing. With a little jolt of confusion rushing through his hammering chest, he twisted around.

Owen was close, a foot away, not much more.

He was dripping wet.

Entirely naked.

Jason had seen most of this before. The broad shoulders and thick, wet chest hair plastered to bronzed skin. Abs that glistened and tapered. Long legs corded with muscle.

What had been a mystery, covered by boxers, was . . . very much unravelled and mere inches from his face.

A curly patch of dark pubic hair surrounded a thick shaft that hung between Owen's thighs, half-mast. Perfectly propor-tioned. It painted a picture of what Owen might have just taken care of, and Jason felt the rising urge to . . . perhaps shower as well. It would be a great way to de-stress after the day they'd had.

Jason blinked, hurriedly jerking his gaze upward. Owen had said something . . . Jason swallowed. "Can you what?"

Owen looked at him with incredible calm and not an ounce of embarrassment. No, all that was rammed into Jason's cheeks. "You're on my towel, sweetheart."

Jason dropped his gaze to the floor with another glance over Owen on the way. His towel. Oh, right. He scrambled off it, tumbling forward in his rush, and Owen had to plant a palm on his forehead, fingers sliding into his hair, to stop him falling against his privates.

"Wow," Jason lifted the towel between them, laughing at himself. "You'd think I'd never been around a naked man before."

"Perhaps just not one you've responded to?" It was a quiet question. No judgements. No teasing.

Jason laughed anyway. He couldn't help it. It was either this or give in to a rather strange urge to sob, and he'd been strange enough this evening already. "Maybe."

Owen's fingers stilled in his hair and slid out again, a soft drag that he felt echo in his toes.

A rough panting sounded, and Jason's eyes widened with horror. "Not me," he said, although his breath was not exactly the smoothest. "Mary."

Somehow, he got to his feet without making more of a fool of himself, and Owen tucked the towel around his waist— something Jason caught reflected in the mirror. He really should try harder not to gawk.

Was the hallway free now? Could he run away?

Owen crowded him toward the door and Jason's breath hitched. Their eyes caught, panicked vs. controlled. "It's all right. I'm here for you. Come."

Owen opened the door, and the strange elation that had sprung up in Jason's veins dissipated. Oh. Of course. He'd been talking to Mary.

Using the doggy distraction, Jason pounded past all hallway inhabitants and threw himself under Owen's bedcovers. Then thought his mad dash might have raised eyebrows and died inside as he called out wantonly, hoping Owen would play along, "Waiting for you, honey."

"Be right there, sweetheart." Good man.

Less than a minute later, Owen, dressed for bed, shut his bedroom door behind him. Jason held his breath and counted a dozen padded footsteps before cooler air funnelled under the blankets and Owen squeezed in beside him. The space was narrow and Jason had left as much of it for Owen as he could, which left him teetering on the edge.

"I'm so sorry," Jason whispered across the darkened pillow. "I only wanted to see you in leotards."

Owen laughed and hauled Jason in by the hips until he was crammed against a shuddering chest. "You got a lot more than leotards."

"A lot *less*, you mean."

"Sure about that?"

Jason considered. "It *was* quite an eyeful."

More laughter shook the bed. Jason's too, this time. Soft cotton and bergamot suffused each breath, and his limbs relaxed, twining between and around Owen's. He looked up, finding Owen's eyes in the dark. "I do have a serious question, though."

Owen tightened his hold. "What's that?"

"Were you humming Rebecca Clarke's 'Piano Trio'?"

Breath whooshed over his temple. "I'd like a list of criteria for what you consider serious, Jason."

"That piece put me on the international stage. Is it one of the things that gave me away? Did you recognise me as a musician?"

"Yes."

A silly wee shiver. Did Owen find music magical? *Jason's* music? "Have you seen me perform?"

"I was at a concert in Melbourne a few years ago. I noticed your uncanny resemblance to Carl then, but dismissed it as coincidence. Only, when you helped Jane with her crossword . . . Adagio. Carl would never have come up with that on the spot. I already had suspicions and then, at the station, I was certain that evening hadn't been a trick of the light. There was another one of him."

"I'm not another him."

"No. No, you are not."

"What was the other thing that gave me away?"

Owen's lips rose at each corner. "You know, I'd love to hear you play again."

Jason thumped lightly against his chest. "Unfair. I'm all taut with suspense."

"Join the club."

A sudden thought. "Is that why you chose Trinity for our date? Were you hoping I'd perform for you?"

"I could see you itching to."

"There were a few moments." His teeth clenched— Hayden, showing off his latest prize in front of the one he'd discarded. "But, you know. Carl."

"Another time, then. When you're not pretending to be your brother."

"How about I bang out something on my instrument tomorrow?"

"Sounds too hot to Handel."

Jason laughed. His fingers flexed and danced on Owen's chest, over his arm, down to his hip. Beethoven. "I'm thinking 'Romance no. 2 in F major'."

"I do like romance."

Jason hummed, continuing to play over Owen, up and down. "Thank you," he murmured as his fingers grew heavy.

"For tonight. All of it." Caring for him at the hospital, taking the blame, not freaking out at Jason's . . . growing curiosity. "You're the most understanding fake boyfriend I've ever had."

"I'm the only boyfriend you've had."

Jason smiled and slipped his fingers under Owen's upper arm. "You must've had a few, though."

"Yes," Owen said slowly.

"Go on."

"The last year at school, before I started at the academy. He tutored me in math."

"Then you tutored him in the ways of love. Jock meets nerd, I can see it. Didn't last?"

"Did I forget to tell you about my other secret boyfriend?"

Jason pinched his nipple, and Owen rumbled with laughter.

"He was heading to uni. We went our own ways."

"Who came next?"

"A distant cousin."

Jason giggled.

"Look, it was a surprise to both of us."

"That Christmas was awkward."

"Needless to say, things got strained, and we weren't in love enough not to care." Owen shifted. "After that, there were a lot of casual hook ups. Until Hayden. No need to scowl."

"I'm not scowling." He was totally scowling. He cleared his throat. "Tell me that story."

Owen pressed his lips together, humming, then, "He was dog-sitting part-time and there was a leash incident at the park which . . . anyway, I got called over, and he was running around laughing, trying to corral the dogs, and I helped. The next day he thanked me again, sans dogs."

"Sounds romantic." Jason began a new tap-tapping rhythm over Owen's chest.

"I fell hard and fast. Two years later, it was all over. I never quite understood."

Fingers softened. "I'm sorry."

"Life seems to have other plans for me."

"You're taking it too well."

"*Now*, I am. Yes."

"Would you get back with him if he came begging?"

A long pause. Very long. Then, "You're really pounding out that tune on me."

Jason drew his hand back. "You know what? Enough about the past. What does your future look like? What do you want?"

"I want to be happy, like everyone."

"What makes you happy? Other than cuffing people."

"There's more to being a cop than cuffing people."

"I didn't mean as a cop."

"How can you be so sure I'm into cuffing?"

"Call me imaginative?"

"Not hopeful?"

Wow, was it hot in here? He fanned the sheets. "Back to being happy, what does that look like for you?"

"Spending time with my family, hanging out with my husband at weekends after we've groaned our way through the weekly chores. Beach visits with Mary. Hikes into the woods. Getting coffees, reading books, travelling once or twice a year. Growing the family."

"Growing the family?"

"Another pup. Maybe a foster kid or two."

Jason's throat tickled. "Not adopt?"

Owen was studying him through the layers of darkness. "Would adopting be a bad thing?"

"N-no. My parents were wonderful. They gave me . . . everything." Jason sat up, stomach roiling. They truly had given him everything he needed. He palmed his forehead.

"You okay?" Owen sat up too, stroking his back like Jason would polish ivory.

"Oh God. I'm an ungrateful, terrible person."

"You're no such thing."

"I loved my parents. Why am I here, so curious to see a part of me that doesn't matter?"

"You can love your parents and still want to know the *what ifs* of life. Hell, how many nights do I wonder what my life would be like if Hayden had moved in? Would we be getting married this year? Would we have talked like this, about what the future could look like?"

Jason fell back to the bed and stared at the ceiling, and Owen stretched himself out beside him. "You're right."

"I know."

Laughter, and Jason batted Owen's chest. He turned on his side and hooked his chin on his palm. "I'm here, like a fly on the wall, for a glimpse."

"Just for a glimpse?"

"I think it feels so urgent because . . . I miss having family around. I'm in a lonely place in my life." He laughed at himself. "Jesus, sorry for unloading that on you."

"I'm your boyfriend. Your bags are mine to carry too."

Jason didn't think it was possible to lose his sense of gravity while lying down. "Owen . . ."

Owen clasped his hands under his head. "Hm?"

"I can see it, you know. Man of law by day, man of the house by night. Stroppy teenager giving you all their sass. You locking them up behind bars until they apologise . . . The narrowed eyes, the see-who-blinks-firsts, the burned toasts while you're chasing another toddler into pants, all the driving to soccer matches, Friday night takeouts, movie nights with fights over who gets to hold the popcorn, the uncountable times you'll laugh every day." The images were vivid. Bright. A lot like how he grew up. "All the times Mary will yip. It'll be out of control, Owen. It'll be perfect. You'll be perfect."

"No one's perfect."

"Then you'll be pretty damn close."

"You are way too good for my ego."

"I'm fond of stroking it."

"Jesus. Okay, my turn to ask a question. I'm your first boyfriend, but you've been with others . . ."

"No one serious until Caroline."

"Was it Caroline's parents who were tragically blind and didn't see how amazing you are?"

Jason laugh-yawned. "Thanks. Yes. I knew from the start we weren't right for one another, but I wanted us to be?"

"You did?"

"I liked her. But more . . ." he dropped his voice. "I liked the *idea* of her? Of having someone who would be there. Who I could have adventures with. Who would love me back." A tight laugh. "She didn't though. I'm not sad about losing her or that she's engaged now, but I'm envious."

"I get that. And that's the third time you've yawned. Sleep time."

"You haven't asked me what my future looks like."

A whisper, "What does your future look like?"

On another yawn, Jason said, "Y'know, I think it looks just like yours."

HE WOKE DRAPED OVER BLANKETS AND OWEN, AN URGENT morning predicament rubbing along a thick arm. Ah, not an arm.

Thank God Owen was still sleeping, boneless, slack-jawed, chest rising and falling steadily under Jason's.

Swallowing a hiss, he delicately uncrossed their swords, and extracted himself to the bathroom with his phone. He showered but couldn't bring himself to . . . not here, with Owen's parents next door. He let cold water rush over him until he was shivering and tried not to flash back to last night as he towelled off and redressed.

Then he collapsed onto the fluffy toilet seat and made his call.

"I'm what?" Carl said, hyperventilating down the line. "*Owen Stirling?* Of all the guys in Tasmania?"

"What's wrong with that?"

"No one will believe you! Can you pull this off? Me and *Owen?* Do you know how many tickets he's given me?"

"He could give you a sight more and I'd still think the world of him."

Carl made a choking sound. "Are you . . . is this . . ."

"Look, he knows the truth. He's able to help me out when I start to go off-script. This is good for both of us."

"Good for . . ." Carl breathed out deeply, and spoke with more calm. "I hope they don't reckon you're pulling a prank."

"They don't so far." Right? They didn't. All the parents had been genuinely eager to see him and wholly supportive.

Or were *they* acting?

He pushed those worries aside. "How're things for you in Wellington? Anything I need to know about? Post?"

Carl got unusually quiet.

"Carl?"

"Oh, look at the time. I've gotta go. Later."

Jason frowned at his phone and jumped at a knock on the door. "Anyone in there?"

Owen's mum.

Quickly, Jason freed the space and followed directions to get the kettle on in the kitchen.

The china cabinet baited him in a shaft of morning light. But attempting to sneak a peek at those photos had gotten him in a lot of trouble last night, and he didn't fancy things getting more out of control this morning . . .

Steam billowed out of a screaming kettle.

What if he opened the drawer an inch? If he got a glimpse, hooray, if not, it wasn't meant to be?

He stole toward the cabinet.

"Morning, Carl."

Jason swung around, guilt a living thing climbing up his neck. Nathan, dressed, cap on, Mary at his side.

"I was just making tea?"

Mary whined, which was rather lenient.

Laughter. "I like you, boy. You're a nice energy. A little mischievous, which I can get behind. Tea bags are in *that* cupboard, though."

Jason turned around, found the Earl Grey, and made tea. They took their mugs out to the sunroom and settled into wicker chairs. In a corner, a cello and a violin rested in their cases, next to creased sheet music on a well-used stand. "Who plays?"

"Me and my daughter. A shared hobby, though lately . . ."

A third figure came into the room, fresh-faced, dark hair streaming around her shoulders. Jason jerked stiffly upright. When would he stop acting so awkward around his birth mother?

He forced himself to relax into his chair and gave her a chin nod. "Cora."

She looked at him funny as she joined them.

Too far in the other direction! Owen! He could do with a little guidance right now. A manly throat-clearing. A distraction.

"I helped myself to some tea, hope you don't mind." Cora eyed the instruments and sipped. "I love classical music." She inclined her head toward Jason. "Tried to get Carl here into the piano. Even bought him a wee beast. But he never took to it."

She'd bought the piano? She'd tried to get Carl . . .

Coincidence? Or had she maybe . . . watched Jason's life quietly and thought if Carl could play, maybe they'd be united in some way?

Jason stared at his tea, quietly laughing at himself. *That was a bit far-fetched, mate.*

"Owen never practiced either, but he is our number one fan. Comes to all our recitals."

Jason looked over at the wide smile under the tartan cap's shadow. "He does?"

"The thing about my son is he's loyal to the bone, and it doesn't take him long to fall in love with things, whether that's music, or an abandoned puppy he found on the beach." He patted Mary's head. "And since Hannah's divorce, he's taken on more responsibility for his nephew. He cares deeply, always has. It's why . . ." He trailed off.

Jason perched onto the edge of his chair. "Why, what?"

An adjustment of his cap. "Why it was so hard on him when Hayden left. He would've given that man forever."

"He didn't deserve it!"

Why he was standing up to announce this, sloshing tea over Owen's T-shirt, Jason couldn't quite say. He'd felt the pain Hayden must have put Owen through and it had gripped him violently. Perhaps there were echoes of the story that reminded him of when Caroline had left, but worse, because Owen had believed he was in love. Jason had futilely hoped he was.

Cora's head cocked inquisitively. "I've never seen you like this before."

Stiffly, Jason set his tea on a side table.

Nathan was eyeing him strangely.

Even Mary was cocking her head. Fantastic.

He had to repair this, and fast. "That's because . . . because . . ."

Renee and Patricia squeezed into the sunroom, heads together, laughing. Behind them, dressed in last night's jeans and T-shirt, Owen tipped himself against the doorframe. His gaze swept over their families and landed firmly on Jason.

"Because," Jason said, slinking across the room between the 'mums' and stopping in front of Owen. "I've never felt like this."

Dark eyes met his. There were a few dozen questions in those eyes, probably along the lines of *What out-of-control shenanigan have we got ourselves into this time?* Questions tempered by the hint of amusement crinkling his eyes.

God, that arched brow. From the moment he'd first seen it, Jason had responded. A sort of rippling shiver in his stomach. A rippling shiver that had only expanded every time he'd seen it since.

Jason smiled up at him. He couldn't help it.

Owen smiled back and there was some magic playing between them that drew Jason close, closer. Soundless music, quavers stringing them together.

A light touch at his side. The shock of a thumb stroking along his hip bone, exposed under the stretched cotton of an old T-shirt.

His pulse rapped a more exuberant beat.

Such dark eyes.

Jason reached a hand around Owen's nape and drew him down. Softly expelled breath hit his nose, the bow of his lip, and Jason's knees quivered. A supportive palm rested knowingly on his thigh, another on his waist, and Jason nudged himself into the hold, a couple of inches closer, against Owen's chest, a warm groin combing his lower stomach.

Jason inhaled that inviting scent, softened by last night's shampoo. Vanilla, honey. Earl grey.

Somewhere in the back of his mind was an awareness of family watching them, and a reminder this moment was for them. For credibility.

Except, it was the curiosity part of him that took up most of his mental space. And there was a flicker in Owen's eyes that said he recognised it.

That perception was a relief to Jason. He liked the electric feeling of Owen reading him, knowing what he wanted. The tightening pressure around his waist guided him. *It's okay. You're doing just fine so far. Keep going. I'll help you.*

He let out a shuddery breath, the tingle of his lips making him swipe his tongue over them. His first kiss with a man. Would he like it?

Would he be good enough at it?

He sucked in a breath, eyes widening. What if he messed up the pressure, the angle, the timing. What if it looked like a first kiss and he gave them away. What if—

A hand slid up his back, coaxing him closer. Their noses grazed. The heat of their mouths mingled.

He'd never trembled so hard.

"Owen?" he whispered, a plea.

Owen kissed him.

Earnest Point Police
@earnestpointcops

Good morning to everyone,
except those who reckon egging
a patrol car is a good idea.

Chapter Eleven

Jason had always thought kissing was . . . good. Fine. Okay, really. He preferred it when lips travelled down his neck, a slick mouth sucked at his throat, teeth grazed his shoulder. Actual pressing of mouths and the plunging of his tongue into hers had always felt . . . a little out of his comfort zone. It made kissing a bit of a chore.

Not this kissing.

All the hard work came from Owen. Guiding hands, the pressure at their lips, the first gentle swipe of tongue. Jason was being steered, and it felt . . . more intense, somehow. Intimate. Like someone saying *I want a taste of what it's like to be inside you,* and the shivery power of being the gatekeeper, deciding if and when to let them in.

In the space of seconds, Owen's lips shifted against his, hot, imploring.

Jason opened for him. A tiny moan.

And then it all disappeared, and air shivered around his mouth, and he was left with a jarring sense that it hadn't been enough. He wanted more teeth, more tongue, more tender desperation.

But, ah . . . probably less audience.

Oh my God, had he *moaned* in front of all the parental units?

He glanced around to four sets of wide eyes.

In a frantic wee move, he started to push away from Owen, but Owen's grasp doubled, keeping Jason tight against him. "Good morning to you, too." Owen swivelled Jason out of the doorway, and out of sight.

As soon as he released him, Jason understood why he'd held on tight those extra moments.

It was one thing to moan in front of four family members.

It was another to spear them with the sight of his very hard, very erect member.

He slapped a hand over his still-singing lips to stifle a yelp of mortification.

Owen's eyes twinkled, a dimple deepening at his cheek. "It's okay," he mouthed, and then louder, "Better get ready. You'll have Jane grumpy if you don't open on time. It's donut day at the station and it'll be a slow trip back after the storm."

THE KISS WOULD NOT LEAVE JASON'S MIND. IT STUCK THERE, AT the forefront, with an intensity that echoed to his most sensitive places. He was throbby, and restless, and he couldn't stop smiling.

Oh crikey.

He wasn't quite sure how to broach the topic with Owen, but he felt quite certain it needed broaching. As soon as possible. And his lips needed breaching. Again.

If Owen didn't mind.

He *hoped* he didn't mind. He'd seemed very easy about the kiss and had taken all of it—and the effects of it—with good humour. Jason had started the morning embarrassed, but . . .

not for long? Owen had taken him in his arms outside the convenience store and dropped another kiss on his forehead. All a bit of show for Cora, of course, but it also felt comforting. Like Owen wanted him to know he didn't care. Jason could relax, be entirely himself. In fact, he'd prefer it.

So if he was upfront about how . . . achy he was feeling, maybe Owen would know what to do about it?

Jane frowned at him as she came up to the counter with her donuts. "Something's off about you, Carl."

Jason just sort of grinned stupidly some more.

She struck a finger in the air. "I know what it is."

Okay, *that* had him reining in half his sunshine. He cast a look over Jane's shoulder to Cora at the magazine stand, flanked by two young red-haired girls bouncing on the balls of their feet. "Y-you do?"

Jane opened her mouth—

"Please, not here?"

She blinked at Jason's harried request and glanced around at Cora. "I'd reckon your cousin would be pleased you're not collecting so many fines?"

Jason ran a hand through his hair. Gosh. Now he'd gotten weird for nothing. "I mean . . . I have a reputation to uphold?"

Jane rang out a teasing laugh. "Jesus, Carl." She studied him and her face pinched with seriousness. "Word of warning. He's strong, but it doesn't mean he can't hurt."

The shift in topic was swift and ruthless. It had him on edge, and that was probably the point. "Sorry?"

"Owen's not just my work colleague, he's my friend. If he so much as lets out a sad grimace, I'll be on your balls."

That sounded pleasant.

"Don't worry," Jason assured her, "We're definitely on the same page."

"It's all happening so quickly," she murmured. "Just like with Hayden."

Except it wasn't. Owen was just kindly helping him out of a tight spot. *Pretending* they'd suddenly and fiercely fallen in love.

Completely different.

"Hayden's an arsehole."

She turned to leave. "As long as he's the only arsehole."

Jason felt his anger rising. The next time he saw Hayden, God. He'd . . . he'd . . . something. He scowled into the middle distance and suddenly Owen was before him with a bottle of milk.

A rumbling laugh. "What's that look for?"

"Owen!" He jerked. "I thought you had stuff to do at home?"

"I was out of milk, and . . . I missed the air of chaos. About that look—"

Jason reached across the counter, balled a hand in soft T-shirt, and hauled Owen into a kiss. Of course, Owen could easily have resisted the move, but he didn't. He folded in and at Jason's small gasp at the electric touch, took over with a warm hum. The flicker of tongue, the press of Jason's top lip sandwiched between his.

Slowly, Jason pulled back.

Owen raised a brow.

"We'll talk about it later," Jason promised.

Cora chuckled, drawing his attention. She was crouching now, a magazine splayed open in her hands, two kids peering at it with her.

"Read mine, read mine," one of them said. "I'm Sagittarius!"

Cora smiled softly. "I know. It's one of my favourite signs."

"It is?"

Cora glanced at him and away, and Jason stilled under the punch of emotion. He wanted the look back. The rawness of it. The pain. The *love*. "I know a Sagittarian. They turned out to be really wonderful. Very good at music."

Wonderful. Good at music.

He sank onto his stool, trying to swallow the lump forming in his throat, blink back the sting in his eyes at the idea she'd kept tabs on him.

Was there a part of her that wished she knew Jason? Wished she could be something to him, even if she could never claim the role of parent? Or even cousin?

"I want to turn out wonderful," the girl said, and Cora smiled at her.

"I'm sure you will."

The other, older girl pushed the magazine closer. "Read it."

Jason felt the prickle of Owen's gaze and it was . . . too much. He was too exposed. He liked Owen understanding him, but *curiosity* was one thing. This . . . he didn't even understand this himself. He was acting weird, quiet and sullen, and he, um, didn't want Owen witnessing his erratic behaviour?

Being put off by it.

Jason had asked him to put up with enough as it was.

He pulled up a grin and hoped it didn't wobble. He jerked a thumb toward the window. "There's a car with no plates out there. You should check it out."

Mary made her presence known with a yip, and Owen held his eyes two beats longer before he led Mary out to 'investigate' the obvious lie.

Too perceptive.

He'd make it up to him. Dinner—the one he'd wanted to impress their parents with—and then take him back to Carl's and bang about on his instrument. An entire symphony all the way to the most exquisite climax.

". . . and Sagittarius will get into quite a few mishaps!"

The girls giggled and Jason smiled fondly too.

"Anything *good?*"

"Yes," Cora said. "No matter what mess you find yourself in, there will always be someone who has your back."

"That's me," said the older sister.

"And me," Cora murmured.

"Cora?" a shy, inquisitive tone.

"Mmm?"

"Are you and Daddy in love?"

The magazine slipped off Cora's hands. The younger girl caught it.

"He wants you to be our new Mummy. Will you?"

Cora's face grew ashen. Her smile looked grim. "I . . . I . . ."

"Daddy has a secret plan for your anniversary."

"Daddy will get mad if you tell her!"

"But Patty is babysitting. She has to know she's going out Saturday."

"Just shush."

The girls scowled at one another, and Cora swallowed hard. Jason had been in enough awkward moments to recognise when someone wanted the world to swallow them up and stop asking questions. He surged to his feet and crossed to them. "Horoscope time, is it?" he called out. "Can you read Libra's out to me?"

"Are *you* a Libra?" The older girl narrowed her eyes at him.

He shook his head. "My boyfriend is, and I'm fairly sure there's a nuisance in his life. What does it say? It's for next week, right?"

The younger girl checked and nodded, then found the Libra symbol and passed the magazine to her sister to read. Cora rose to her feet, swiping at her eyes, a sudden laugh falling from her painted lips. "Libra is in a good position to make a beautiful match," she said, and looked at him.

"Yes, it says here: Libra couples," the girl read aloud, a little stilted in places. "Romantically, you're in the front seat, and you should expect to drive the way to upcoming relationship milestones. There are a few blind corners to come, and the destination is unclear. For single Libras," she paused. Technically, *Owen* was a single Libra . . . Jason paid close attention. "Old lovers will return and new passions may be reignited. Light and fun sexy times are highly likely."

He frowned.

Cora mistook his expression. She grimaced, "Um, so not quite child-friendly, that horoscope. I probably shouldn't have given you that magazine. Does this make me a bad—" She stopped, laughing hollowly. "Of course I am. Rightio, kids, Daddy will be back any minute. Let's wait outside."

She herded the kids towards the door, and Jason stopped her in her tracks. She looked at him quizzically, and he raised his hand.

Her expression crumpled and her hand met his, shaking. The press of their fingers felt fraught with emotion and the look she left Jason with . . .

He rubbed his chest, found the magazine, and read his birth mother's horoscope.

A huge opportunity looms before you, Gemini. If you find yourself doubting your ability to do it justice, repeat the mantra: You can do it. If you're still unsure, look around you. The universe is rooting for you. With the right courage, past, present, and future just might collide and forge something beautiful.

He thought . . . he understood the opportunity.

Her pained look at him, though. She didn't, couldn't believe she'd be allowed it.

He frowned over it all day.

Took the problem back home.

To dinner.

To the keys of Carl's newly tuned piano, melting under his touch . . .

Music lifted into the air, soft, rounded, a slow dance from

light to dark. He stopped abruptly and turned to Owen, on an armchair in the living room behind him. The lamps cast his shadow over the rolling sea of ivory.

Sergeant Owen Stirling Sir leaned forward, forearms on his knees, hands clasped together, gaze locked on him, waiting.

"I'm too restless for this." Jason stood and paced the rug. "It feels wrong, playing in this house. I should be playing in yours."

A flash of something hit those dark eyes, and Jason paced some more, coming nearer to Owen bit by bit, like spiralling to a mountain top. His breath was becoming more laboured too. "I've got . . . things on my mind."

"What kind of things?"

Jason stopped in front of him, toe to toe, and Owen leaned back in the chair, looking up. Relaxed, easy. Unconcerned about what Jason might say, like he'd take anything. Such a rock.

"I want to tell you something." He bit his lip, worrying it.

Owen reached out and tugged him into his lap. Jason crumpled atop him, knees sliding either side of Owen's thighs with a bounce that had him catching his breath. Owen's hands slid around his hips, holding him steady, and dark eyes met his. "You can tell me anything."

"Wow, you are such a great boyfriend."

Owen sat up, bringing their bodies closer. "You're quite something yourself, Jason." The soft words fell like a caress.

"Am I?" He was fishing. Yes. Desperately. But after Caroline, he hadn't come away with confidence in his boyfriending abilities.

"You cook, you help keep the house clean, you engage so warmly with my family, you give to my nephew without expectation of anything in return, you're hardworking, you're playful. You know how to make me laugh. You *really* know how to make me cry." Owen said that last part with a smirk; and true.

There'd been a few things to cry about. Like how much of a magnet for disaster he was.

Jason grinned back at him. "I'm afraid there's more where that all came from."

Owen leaned forward, whispering, "I can't wait." He slipped one of his hands up Jason's back and squeezed his nape, his fingertips pressing into the base of his scalp, pushing him closer. Their noses bumped. "What do you want to tell me, Jason?"

"I-I'm kind of nervous."

"That's okay. Take all the time you need."

Slowly, shudderingly, he released his breath. "It's . . . it's about . . ."

"Cora?"

Jason blinked. Owen knew?

"Something upset you today. You've been frowning all evening, and your music was incredible, but also incredibly sad."

"All those deduction skills. You must be a really good cop."

"You're stonewalling."

"There you go, proving my point."

"Jason . . ."

Jason let out a breathy laugh that turned into a sigh at its peak. "I promised I wouldn't tell anybody, but it's so much on my chest."

Owen hummed. "You were worried last night with Patricia, but the way you look at her and the way you look at Cora . . ." Owen focused on him, puzzle pieces coming together. A probable conclusion filling his eyes.

Jason blinked back the sting in his eyes. Nodded. "Yes."

"And Patricia?"

"Only wanted to have one of us."

Owen breathed in Jason's shuddered exhale. "I'm sorry."

"I'm . . . not. I'm not angry or hurt. Cora was fifteen, she did what she thought was best. I had a great mum and dad. I never missed . . . But I was curious what might have been. I *am* curious. That word again." He laughed, a tear spilling. "I'm a cat. Let's hope it doesn't kill me."

Owen thumbed the tear over his cheekbone. "It's okay to be curious."

"Is it? I'm curious about *all sorts of things*, Owen." He laughed at himself again. Owen caught his chin and drew his attention to dark eyes.

"That's okay too."

"Even if I'm achy and restless?" His ears were undoubtedly turning pink. "Even if I want to . . . I mean, only if you want to. I understand if you think this complicates things."

"They're already complicated."

Jason laughed. He'd made a mess, all right. "In two weeks this will all be over."

Owen looked . . . unconvinced.

"You're right." Jason sagged against him and tucked himself close with a wee laugh that he hoped didn't show his disappointment. "Anything more might be too much."

Owen lifted Jason off his lap and steered him out of the house.

"What?" Jason asked. "Have I reached your limit again?"

"Surpassed it."

"Um, but you're steering me to your place?"

"Yes. You're sleeping with me."

"Or Mary and the guestroom will be fine."

"No," Owen said, "I'm not being clear." He crowded against Jason's back, a wall of heat in the cool evening. He reached around him to unlock his door. A whisper combed Jason's ear. "You're not sleeping *with* me." A gentle smack on his arse had Jason stepping over the threshold and spinning around. Owen collided with him, a wave of purpose and knee-buckling intention. "You're sleeping under me."

Earnest Point Police
@earnestpointcops

Overtaking a cop car going
seventy in a fifty zone, probably
not your cleverest idea.

Chapter Twelve

Owen didn't let any second thoughts come between them and Jason came to life, one breath shock, the next all warmth. He drew back an inch, searched Owen's fiery brown eyes, and then cupped his nape, steering those soft, insistent lips back to his.

Steady, guiding hands urged Jason against the wall. Owen kicked off his shoes and prowled Jason down the hall. There was something fresh about the confidence with which Owen moved. Mary yipped, and Owen told her to stay in the lounge, a gentle command that promised he knew exactly where he wanted this to go, and how to get Jason there.

And Jason was definitely up for the ride.

Two giddying steps. Three.

Bedroom.

Dresser, mirror, shelves bathed in moonlight. Cool breezes wisped through an open window. Curtains aflutter. Like his heart.

The backs of his knees hit the side of the bed and gravity shot through him as he fell to the mattress.

Owen pushed his arms over thick cotton and rough

stitching and clasped Jason's wrists in one hand. Jason's heart pounded and he made a noise, a broken syllable, possibly Owen's name. Definitely a plea.

Owen stretched out over him, taut and hard, and Jason sucked in bergamot. Lavender. A raw moan, low and rumbly.

"Shoes off."

Jason complied, a push of a heel against the bedframe, another against the back of Owen's calf. Sneakers hit the floor.

Knees drove between his legs, swift and sure, pushing his thighs apart. Even with their pants on it was the most intense sexual moment of Jason's life. Like their kisses, Owen made every electrical spark *sing*—and right now he was all sparks.

Jason arched up against that sweet, intense grind. "Oh my God, Owen."

"Hmm?"

"Crazy intense."

Nibbles down his throat.

"Owen, I'm serious."

"Too much?"

Owen started to draw away and Jason lifted his legs to lock him in place. He stared into those dark eyes. "Why does it feel like this?"

"Like what?"

"Fierce, like . . . like Rachmaninov. 'Prelude in c-sharp minor'."

The way Owen looked at him—those darkening eyes, their focus dropping to Jason's lips . . .

His pulse was all semi-quavers.

He wanted more. Wanted everything, every touch—soft, sensual, strong, frantic—

He jerked his wrists against Owen's hold. Owen raised a brow. "What would you like?"

"Buttons. Undone."

Owen slid a hand tight between them, stroking him through his jeans. "These buttons?"

Jason growled at him.

A lusty laugh.

He seemed to be getting Owen off too. That was . . . thrilling. Made it even better. He'd always strived for harmony in sex, with his girlfriends, and they'd never quite reached it. All the notes there, but in the wrong . . . key. Flat. Not sharp, like this.

Owen stroked over him again. *Tease.*

"What's the smile about, Jason?"

Breathless, "Get me out and I'll tell you."

"How about I make you come in your pants?"

Jason groaned through another slide down his shaft. "If you must know, I was thinking how very un-Libra like you're being. You're not playing fair at all, Sergeant Owen Stirling Sir."

Owen kissed him hard, fingers plucking eagerly at buttons, then more eagerly taking hold of him. A firm grasp. A gentle pull.

Jason hissed and threw his head back, baring his throat.

Owen scraped his teeth there, sucked, drawing all sensation to that one spot. C in the eighth octave. The highest note.

It vibrated through him to his balls, and like Owen *knew*, he squeezed his cock. Like lengthening sound with a pedal. Jason clenched his thighs around Owen's hips, breathless with the singing ache of it. He wanted to squirm under this touch forever.

Air tunnelled between them and drifted down his back as the room shifted. Owen had moved him. A thin pillow supported his neck now. His hands had been freed, and—

Oh.

Jason shivered at the solid slide of Owen's exposed shaft

against his. Hard and hot and damp. Oh God, could his clothes please come off?

A laugh. "All right."

Already so far gone. Had to be if he was moaning his inner thoughts aloud. Whatever. Free him. Fuck him.

"You're robbing me of reason. Christ."

"Reason? If you're still thinking straight, you're doing it wrong."

"I promise, I'm not thinking straight."

For some reason, Jason found that particularly amusing. He laughed heartily as he yanked off his shirt and Owen stripped him of his jeans, all light and ticklish over his legs. He watched Owen shimmy out of his own until they were fully exposed on fresh, moonlit blankets. What was usually an awkward moment during sex felt . . . freeing. The shift of material. Glorious gold-dusted thighs, calves. Naked feet. The tossing of his T-shirt onto the floor. Rippling muscle and purpose.

Holy *hell*. Calendar cop!

Owen's shadow loomed over him. Their skin touched a clash of notes in the high octaves. Balls rested against throbbing balls. Jason clasped the globes of Owen's arse and dug his nails in. "Show me?"

"You're in a candy store, aren't you?"

"I want everything." Flushed, "Is that allowed?"

Owen paused for half a second. A fraction of a second. "Yes."

A wave of relief rolled through him. He wanted to try other stuff too, of course, but he really, really wanted to let Owen *in*, like he had with their kisses—that slick breaching. And he wanted it now so if he liked it, they could do more of it in the short time they had. "Thank God. Now fuck me."

Owen's eyes glimmered. A twitch of his lip. "You're quite bossy, aren't you? Waltzing into my life and claiming all my attention, moving in, hounding after photos, telling me what to do in bed."

He hadn't thought of himself like that before, but . . . he could see how he had some demanding tendencies . . . "Maybe I tell you what to do. But *how* you do it . . . that's all up to you."

"Anything else I should have in mind?"

A shaky laugh. "I'm a little nervous, so . . . like a Band-Aid?"

He expected there to be some pain, but pain wasn't the worst thing in the world. He could handle it. Especially if what came after transposed him from this mortal realm to somewhere magical. "By that I mean . . . plunge."

Owen frowned down at him. "I'm not going to hurt you."

Jason swallowed. He wasn't quite sure where to put that sincerity. It sort of flapped about, butterflies in his chest that wouldn't calm down. "Upgrade that to very nervous, Owen."

A wolfish grin. That placed itself easily—right at his cock. "Anticipation is all part of it."

"W-what's that look for? What are you planning?"

"Don't worry. You'll thank me for it." Owen was sliding down Jason, gently spreading his legs apart, guiding Jason's hands to his knees to hold himself open.

Heat flashed through Jason, lingering in his cheeks, in his rigid cock.

"Stay like that." Owen got off the bed, moved to his drawers, and returned to kneel between Jason's legs.

Jason's fingers slipped on his knees and he changed his grip, thighs falling higher. Owen's gaze rushed over him, from head to toe to centre. Empowering, seeing Owen visibly shiver, reach for his cock and tug like he couldn't help himself. Rip open the lube and dollop some on those large blunt fingertips.

Jason rocked on his arse, the cool air and that wanton look stirring him silly with need.

"I got you, sweetheart," Owen said, and cool gel met his

opening, a gentle slide down. The tip of a thumb teasing the rim.

Oh hell. More of that.

"P-please."

Owen swore, and it was satisfying to feel his fingers shake as they pushed into him. Tiny movements, over and over. Slowly, God so slowly, slipping in further. A merciless tease.

A whine, "*Owen*."

Fingers grew frantic, and they both groaned. Jason slammed his head back on that pillow—

Wet, slick heat slid over his straining cock; Jason let out a cry and dropped his knees as he bucked up into the intense feel of Owen's tongue and tight, squishy throat. The sting and stretch of slippery fingers came in and out of him deeply now, and he loved the juxtaposition. Both ends of the piano playing at once. He pulled Owen off his cock and surged up, kissing those raw lips. "More?"

Owen kissed him with slow, measured control, lips locking, tongue sliding into him like a prelude to what was coming. Oh God, deep, like that. Yes.

Fingers disappeared and there was a crinkle of foil.

Owen pulled out of the kiss, dark eyes blackened with arousal. "Jerk yourself while I sink into you."

He grasped Jason's knees, bringing them to rest against his shoulders. He settled close, so close. Closer than Jason had imagined, and it added a layer of intimacy between them he hadn't expected. He was throbbing and needy, a little flushed from the exposure of it all, and now the air thickened and awareness crept over him.

Owen shifted forward, and the slick end of his cock nudged a billion nerve-endings.

Jason sucked in a shivery breath. It felt . . .

He'd never done this with a man before. He'd begged Owen to be the one to show him what it could be like. And

Owen, so obliging. In the hottest, most controlled way imaginable. Jason had told him just to plunge in, but Owen held back his own pulsing pleasure to open him carefully.

Considerate. Thoughtful.

Jason looked away, gravity swooping around his chest.

Owen steered Jason's chin back.

Their eyes met, and Owen pushed inside him.

His hand trembled on Owen's shoulder. Owen gasped, muscles straining as he held himself steady, slowly, inch by inch, stretching him, filling him.

"God, you feel . . . so tight. So good around me."

The rawness of his words, the intense pleasure over Owen's face. Jason wanted to give him more, to take every inch of him in. Wanted to service every wish Owen had of him.

The thought had him rock hard, lifting his hips to help Owen slide deeper.

Oh God. Oh *God.*

He clenched, feeling . . . feeling obscenely full, taken, *needed.* The desire in Owen's eyes, the slackened jaw, the rolling eyes.

His heart banged against his chest.

Owen rocked.

A clash of cymbals.

Music behind his shuttering eyes.

He sang out a moan.

Owen dipped down and kissed him, then pulled himself out and made Jason sing again.

It was different from any other sex he'd had. Owen's shifts hit a place inside of him he'd never felt before. The nerves at his ring. Those magnificent ones inside . . . He had to let go of his cock or he'd explode.

He was right to ask for everything right away. Too delicious. Another stratosphere of pleasure. He'd want this over and over.

Owen set a relentless pace of powerful thrusts that made

music of him. Moan after moan. His whole body prickled, on fire. He threaded fingers through blond hair, banged his heels against the contracting muscles in Owen's back.

Gravelly, awed, "Look at you, Jason."

Jason lifted his head. Owen was large over him, rippling muscle sheened with sweat; his cock appeared, a long fat shaft, and disappeared inside *him*. That was . . . Was . . .

"So *good*." Jason grabbed Owen's face and kissed him eagerly. He wanted more. He was high on it. Like he could never get enough. "Are there other positions? Can we try them?"

A groan, and another thrust into him. "You never bloody cease to surprise me."

Nothing could be as surprising as *this*. "Maybe on my knees with you behind me?"

Owen pulled all the way out and lightly slapped his arse. "Turn around, then."

Jason scrambled onto his knees; Owen palmed his hips, thumbs spreading him, and sank into him with a grunt. *Oh.* If the angle wasn't intense enough, Owen overloaded his synapses by draping his warm body over his cool back and kissing the rising hairs on his nape. He stayed cocooned around him like that, just cocked his hips back and forth in shallow thrusts.

Jason's elbows folded, forearms bracing against the bedspread. Owen looped his arms under his, pinning his hands in place as he quickened his pace. Being restrained like that . . . surrounded . . .

Lips at the crook of his neck, wet tongue running a horizontal line across the base. Jason felt the echo of that collar at his throat.

Possessed . . .

Jason panted, shuddered with each exhilarating smack into him.

This. This had been a fantasy. Something that got him off

wanking in the shower, the thought of being pinned down and taken. It'd been something he tried to explain to Caroline, to others, but it'd never been realised, and Owen—

Owen took him like he knew exactly what Jason wanted.

All that crazy perception.

If they were face to face, he'd kiss him right now. But, no . . . keep drilling him into the mattress. The fleeting grazes of his cock over the sheets, perfect.

Another bite to his neck.

His balls tightened. "Owen . . ." A gasped warning.

"I got you" soft at his ear. Owen fucked him harder, with fierce energy. The bed rocked and butted against the wall, and Jason was a symphony of pounding pleasure—

Violin, viola, cello, double bass, flute.

Owen shifted; air cooled Jason's back. His wrists were ghosted cuffs of pressure.

Oboe. Clarinet. Bassoon.

A tight, squeezing hold at his nape. A seeping cock.

Horn. Trumpet. Trombone.

A groaning gasp.

Tuba! Harp! Celesta!

It burst out of him, wave after thunderous wave.

Piano.

OWEN CAME A FEW THRUSTS LATER WITH A DEEPLY SINFUL grunt that made Jason smile. They collapsed into his sticky pool of come, Owen still inside and sprawled atop him, panting. "God, Jason. That was something else."

"Wasn't it?"

"How are you feeling?"

"Can we do it again?"

"Probably not for a few hours." Light nips at his ear. "Let's be realistic. Tomorrow."

At his forlorn sigh, Owen laughed and slipped out of him. While he knotted and disposed of his condom, Jason twisted and shoved himself onto the dry side of the bed.

"Maybe next time without? I mean, I tested . . . I'm negative."

Owen's gaze snapped to his and held in a way that made his chest flutter again.

"Or whatever," Jason amended, feeling he'd stepped somewhere . . . dangerous. A little beyond his skillset. "I'll do anything you like."

A glance toward the darkened garden; an amused shake of his head. Owen crawled towards him, and Jason instinctively wrapped his arms around Owen's neck and pulled him close. Their noses bumped, and their kiss tasted of sweat, sex, and lavender.

"Your curiosity *will* kill something. Me."

"Your stamina seemed pretty impressive."

Owen groaned and kissed his forehead, then neatly rolled them off the bed. "Let's change the top cover."

"And the pillow slip." As they fluffed out fresh bedding, Jason added, "I hope we have enough spares. I foresee that happening a fair bit."

Earnest Point Police
@earnestpointcops

There are two nicely cleaned public toilets on Kent and Cove. Anyone wanting to glimpse the incredible steel toilet we have down at the station; peeing on your neighbours' fences is a good way to go about it.

Chapter Thirteen

J ason woke up plastered over Owen's body, like he had in his childhood bedroom, hard and wriggling against, well . . . this time he let himself wriggle.

When they'd both grunted out a magnificent morning release, Owen laughingly deposited him in the shower. "You certainly are all endless energy."

Jason grinned under the spray of warm water. "Sagittarius. I told you. Wash my back?"

When they were very, *very* clean, they dressed and flowed into their usual morning routine. Jason cut up fruit into muesli for them, and Owen made coffee.

They sat perpendicular to one another at the square dining table, a pleasant nearness that came with the serenity of not having to speak. Owen liked to read the news on his phone, and Jason jotted out a shopping list. Wrote CORA? in large letters as a single bullet point. And then skipped to the task Pete had given him: find replacement musicians.

He looked up a few options on his phone and penned a few numbers to try, but none of them sounded like great matches.

He glanced over at Owen, in shorts and a loose, old T-shirt. He wanted to mow the lawns, he'd said.

So glad he had the day off to watch . . .

Musicians.

He thought of the violin and cello he'd spotted in the sunroom before the kiss that—

Focus.

"Owen?"

"Hm?"

"Your dad and your sister . . . would they be good enough to play for Pete's wedding?"

Owen hesitated, gaze flickering to him. "Yes, they would."

"Could I ask them?"

Owen set down his phone and leaned back in his chair. "I don't mind, but . . ."

"But I've never met your sister and that would be weird? Yeah, I guess."

"Not where I was going with that." A pause. "Would you like to meet her?"

Jason clickity-clicked his pen. He couldn't lie. He'd been fascinated with everyone else in Owen's family, and he'd like to satisfy his curiosity about Alex's mum. Owen's older *sister*, who played cello. Hannah. "Could I?"

"I wanted to drop in before work today."

"Back to work?"

"Late shift this week. Two to twelve."

Oh. There went a few fantasies of how the evenings would go. On the other hand, he could use that time . . . he should be putting in more piano hours. "Can I stay here? With Mary?"

"Anything you like."

Jason hummed dreamily. "What I'd *really* like is a piano in this room." Maybe over by those windows, if the couch and TV shifted to the other corner. Except . . . even if he *could* rent out a grand piano, it might only arrive when it was time for him to go.

Owen was looking at him over his coffee. Jason shook out of the tangent thought and returned to his pen and paper. "I'll ask Hannah, then."

"You know who would be better than Hannah and my dad?"

He poised the tip of his pen to the next clear line. "Who?"

Owen plucked the pen from his fingers and wrote on the paper.

Jason read and laughed brightly. "If *I* play, there might just be a few people who see through this charade."

Another long sip of coffee. "So what if they did?"

Jason's heart lurched into his throat, pulsing wildly. "Carl—"

"Is a big boy."

"I'd still be letting him down. And Cora . . . Patricia . . . The fallout of this whole town finding out the truth."

"A fallout of some kind will be inevitable."

"I can handle a bit of hurt for the greater good."

"Sure it'll be the greater good?"

"They haven't even told Carl that Patricia isn't his birth mum. Let alone that there's a twin brother running around. They don't want anyone knowing the truth."

"Carl found out anyway. So did I."

The quiet, cop-like inquisition flustered Jason, made him . . . think about it—what it might be like if they knew. Would they accept him or . . . turn away from him again? What if they acknowledged him, but that was it?

He wasn't really theirs to care about, after all.

That kind of rejection . . . No. Better not to expose himself to that. He'd have a few good memories; that would be enough.

He swallowed; his throat felt raw.

"What are you going back to, Jason?" The question was quiet. And stung.

What he was going back to was an echoing house and a barrage of social media posts following Caroline to her wedding day. He was going back to feeling lost.

He stood, laughing hollowly. "More manageable wildlife?"

"Jason . . ."

Owen's softly furrowed brow and that downward crease at the side of his lips started to blur and Jason twisted away, blinking. "Could I borrow your car, please? I want to swing by the supermarket."

～

OWEN DIDN'T SO MUCH AS BLINK AT THE REQUEST. JUST handed him his keys and a spare one to the house, and asked Jason if he thought he'd be done by midday so they could see Hannah before cop-duty called. Jason shopped at Woolworths and swung by the convenience store—run by Carl's part timer on his days off—for a few more things.

The yard was freshly cut by the time he hauled in the supplies, and Owen had vacuumed and mopped inside too.

Mary found Jason filling the cupboards, and Jason rummaged through his bags to the treats he'd bought. "This," Jason said, holding up a beefy doggie snack, "is me bribing you for your love."

She wagged her tail and deftly snatched the flying treat out of the air.

A low laugh had him swinging to Owen and taking a few long moments to . . . appreciate. The way he filled out that uniform . . . the shirt, the pressed pants, the polished shoes . . . where was the utility belt?

"What was that?" he murmured, as the beltless hips approached.

Owen peered into the bags. "Anything to bribe me with?"

"An officer of the law? We've had this conversation. I would *never.*" Jason pulled out a block of roasted almond chocolate. "But doesn't this look delicious?"

Owen gripped one end of it, but Jason didn't let go. He met Owen's warm eyes. "Look . . . sorry about before, I know you're only watching out for me. Thanks for giving me a moment. And for your car."

Owen took the chocolate and set it down, then he stepped up to Jason and cupped his cheek. "I'm sorry too. I have concerns, but they are very much my own. I'll be more respectful going forward."

Jason wanted to kiss him.

So . . . he did.

A light press of their mouths. A thank you. "Do I have time to whip up some apple bran muffins?"

"Sounds delicious."

"They're to take to Hannah's. Wait." He gripped Owen's arm tightly. "Any allergies I should know about?"

THEY PARKED IN HANNAH'S DRIVEWAY NEXT TO CARL'S JEEP, a picket fence, and a square patch of garden edged with roses. They climbed out of the car, Jason clutching his Tupperware of fresh muffins against his stomach.

Owen paused to answer a call as he let Mary out. Watching over the roof of the car, Jason caught the gist. Hannah—she was running a few minutes late.

Jason felt a sigh drop through him. Enough time to settle down and find his inner calm. He gestured to the muffins and made for the porch. "I'll take these inside and say hello to Alex."

He buzzed the doorbell. Heard a thump from inside the house. Knocked. "Alex?"

Footsteps.

The door cracked open. "Carl?"

Jason grinned. "Here to meet your mum. Uh, officially. As, you know, your uncle's boyfriend. Can I come in?"

"Mum's not here!"

"She's on her way."

"*What?* I'm, ah . . ."

Jason finally took in the picture before him. A half-closed door, and Alex peering around the side of it.

"We're in the middle of a study session."

A little step to his right revealed . . . a lot of Alex. With boxers on backwards. "Study session?"

Alex flushed bright red, from head to chest to toe. "Please don't tell Uncle Owen?"

"You're eighteen, Alex—"

A door opened. Two broad men in their early to mid-twenties. Both stark naked. Jason almost dropped his muffins.

Always the quiet ones.

His brow touched his hairline.

Alex glanced over his shoulder and waved his . . . study buddies back into his room.

Quite good-looking guys—"Aren't we showering together?"

But perhaps not particularly perceptive.

Alex shot a horrified glance over his shoulder. "No-no, Mum's coming back. Clothes on!" His gaze pleaded with Jason.

"Owen would understand," Jason whispered.

"He'd go all cop, he's very protective. It's not just . . . we're . . . together. He'd scare them away."

Right. A lot of secrets about boyfriends in this town. Jason pretending to have one, Alex pretending he didn't have two.

The poor kid. He was having a tough time as it was—struggling with studies, trying to help his mum with the mortgage, and now they had to buy out his dad after the divorce. Whatever this was exactly, Alex had it, and his gaze said he needed it.

"Please, Carl?"

Every day got just a bit more complicated.

"Take these."

Alex took the muffins and, at the scuff of footsteps behind him, Jason spun around with a cheery smile. "Such a lovely day." Clouds cast a shadow and drops of light rain fell between them. He fought a grimace. "Nice and fresh. Let's wait for Hannah out here."

Mary rustled out from behind a rose bush and loped towards the door. The *parted* door. She pushed inside, swinging it wide on its hinges.

Distract Owen. Distract him!

Jason flung himself into Owen's rather surprised and fast-reacting arms. *Oof*s were expelled between them, and Owen stared at him shrewdly. "What now?"

Yap, yap, yap.

Oh, Mary Puppins. Please.

"Jason?"

In for a penny . . . he batted his eyelashes. "First of all, I want to make one thing clear: I never explain anything."

Owen stared at him. Dark eyes and firm jaw, a little prickly at the edges, stubble darker where his lip quirked. "Why are you quoting Mary Poppins?"

"It was the first thing that popped into my head?"

"A fan, are you?"

"I watched it in bed that night."

"What night?"

"The day you told me Mary's full name. I figured it'd help me get to know you. You recognised the quote, so I figure I'm on the right track."

A long, hard stare that . . . seemed to make soup of Jason's insides.

"What is it you're not saying?"

Jason stiffened in his arms. "Nothing?"

A reproaching look.

Jason planted a smacking kiss on his lips. "A spoonful of sugar helps the medicine go down?"

Disbelieving laughter, and Owen clutched Jason's hips as if to steer him aside—

Jason tightened his arms around Owen's neck and jumped on him, locking his legs behind his back. Good thing he wasn't wearing the belt. Every other part of his uniform, though.

God, he was molesting a cop. This was . . . possibly not his sanest moment.

He flashed Owen all his teeth. "Nowhere to go but up?"

Owen heaved them both towards the door with impressive strength and co-ordination. "I'll deal with you later, sweetheart."

"Alex! Incoming!"

The walls barely muffled Alex's shriek.

Owen reached the porch.

Jason jabbered, "He's an adult, Owen."

Owen halted at the door, and Jason glanced nervously into the hall. Alex was frantically ushering his boyfriends towards the other end of the house. Socks and briefs on, hopping into jeans, T-shirts slung around their necks. Alex still very much in his backwards boxers.

Owen flushed and palmed the door to brace himself and all Jason's deadweight. The wooden frame pressed into the side of his back, and Owen dropped his forehead to meet Jason's, groaning quietly. "I should've listened to you."

Jason tightened his legs and arms around Owen, a squeeze of sympathy.

"I still see the boy that I took to the beach at the weekends to help train Mary."

"He's still the boy who looks up to you. So be careful, Owen."

"I want to grill those young men."

"Grill me instead. Get it out of your system."

Quiet laughter ghosted over the bridge of his nose.

The sound of a car pulling up on the street had Jason slipping off Owen, and Owen staring down the hall at Alex who stared back like a stunned possum. A mortified stunned possum. "I take it my sister doesn't know?"

"I don't know how to explain it." He grimaced at the sound of something shattering in the bowels of the house. "She was supposed be working."

Owen nodded and turned swiftly toward his sister while Jason gestured Alex to hurry up and get this under control. It was okay that he hadn't told people yet. It was okay that he didn't know how.

It was okay that he needed more time.

Momentarily, Jason's own restlessness eased.

He closed the door and stood at Owen's side in the thickening rain. The nerves he'd had when they arrived at Hannah's soared back to the surface and he clutched Owen's elbow. Owen patted him and murmured, "She'll love you."

Hannah held her hands up like a shield against the raindrops. She jogged up the path, blonde ponytail bouncing, smile growing. She had warm dark eyes, very much like her brother's, although perhaps heavier at the edges. A face that had experienced a lot, but had never forgotten the glow of a grin.

"Carl. Jesus. Dad warned me and I honest to God thought he was having me on." She glanced from him to Owen and whacked his arm. "Kept that quiet, didn't you?"

Jason cleared his throat, "I hope you aren't too upset."

"Upset?" Hannah laughed that off with a wave. "Nah. I

have a philosophy about secrets." She glanced between them, hand still visored at her forehead. "Should we head in?"

Owen stepped aside, making a path for her, and gave Jason a reassuring wink as they followed her to the porch. She opened the door to Mary welcoming her home, tail wagging, and fussed over her just as warmly as her brother.

Alex appeared at the end of the hall, holding his fingers an inch apart while Hannah was bowed over floppy ears. *Almost there.*

She straightened and Owen and Jason spoke at the same time. Owen shook his head with quiet laughter, and Jason bit his lip on a nervous grin.

You go, he mouthed.

"What's your philosophy on secrets?"

Hannah looked between the two of them. "You only feel safe to share secrets if you're loved enough." She kissed Owen's cheek. "And only you know when you feel loved enough."

Loved enough. Safe enough. To share secrets.

Or they got found out. By clever cops who happened to read right through you until the truth just blabbered out. Or he glimpsed it from the porch.

As they moved into the house and other conversations took hold, it was this one that held his real attention. He eyed Owen laughing, gently ribbing his sister before slinging himself next to his nephew and fondly patting his head.

Alex released a breath and dropped against Owen's side, like Jason could imagine him having done as a kid.

Something hummed in his stomach. He thought of how openly his parents had told him he was adopted. How Carl, Cora and Patricia all knew, and didn't say anything.

Cora.

He saw her pained look when the girls had asked if she'd be their new mummy.

She . . . she didn't know just how much Carl loved her. How much he loved her regardless of the truth.

Jason, for all the mess he was making . . . needed to do some fixing. He needed to help Cora *realise*.

"Carl?"

The voice lurched him back to reality. He'd followed Hannah, hard-working, down-to-earth, decent Hannah—a trait that definitely ran in the family—to a room overlooking the back garden. Her cello sat on a stand, and he was fingering the sheet music while Owen and Alex shared a quiet conversation in the lounge, a light murmuring.

"Never thought you had much interest in music."

Jason stiffened, back to her, staring at the sea of notes in front of him. A language he knew better than the back of his hand. Shit. He'd been humming the tune. "I'm full of surprises?"

A breezy laugh. "That you are."

He swallowed. "And, uh, Pete's been asking me to find musicians for his wedding. I thought maybe you and your dad might be interested?"

Owen cleared his throat. He was close; Jason felt the warm buzz. "Sorry to interrupt." Jason smiled softly; he was sure Owen had done so on purpose, to save Jason from giving himself away. Owen looked at him and jerked a thumb in the direction of the living room. "Mary is eyeing your muffin."

Jason took the offered reprieve and hounded after the plate on the coffee table, not hungry at all. He'd shown far too much interest in music back there. Let it distract him, on instinct.

He slouched next to Alex on the sofa.

Alex looked at him, equally miserable, and both their lips started twitching. Jason scrolled a hand through his hair. "Tough work, keeping secrets."

"Yeah." Alex paused. "Thanks for helping me out. You

were right, he doesn't care about the specifics . . . just that I'm okay."

Jason shoulder-bumped him. "We're lucky to have him, aren't we?"

Alex rubbed his nape and peeked at Jason. "He's lucky to have you, too."

Hardly. Landed with Jason's epic spiralling mess of misadventures . . . The man wasn't lucky. He was a saint. "Well, who wouldn't be to have all this?"

Alex giggled; Mary jumped up on the couch between them and licked Jason's face.

~

STRANGE TO GO FROM ALL THAT COMPANY TO CRUISING AROUND in Owen's car, alone. They left Mary with Alex, and Jason had accompanied Owen to the station, Owen insisting Jason take the car—go check out the area, do something nice for himself. He'd take a patrol car home tonight.

"You're allowed to do that?"

"After a late shift, yeah. It's fine. We're rural, some things that might be frowned on in the city aren't out here."

Jason slunk his attention down his chest and lingered at his hips. "Will you be coming home in a belt? In that enormously intimidating belt holding up your important instruments?"

A groan. "Eyes up so close to the station, sweetheart." Fingers steered his chin up toward a slow, simmering smirk. Owen handed the car keys over the console. "Have a good day. Night too, if you're sleeping when I get back."

"I mean," Jason bit his lip. "You can wake me? It must be very hard getting out of the belt—"

Laughing, "No belts. I like my job." A pause. "Some cuffs on the other hand . . ."

Owen slipped out of the car, and Jason watched his backside all the way to the station doors. Sighed, and double-checked the message threads on his phone.

Cora: Sorry, not at home today.

Carl: Cora's? 49 Gum Drive. Key under the flowerpot on the porch. I always let myself in.

Right, got it. Good. He headed for Gum Drive, making a stop on the way, then swung a left into the cosy cul-de-sac and slowed to a crawl.

One of these houses was Cora's . . . Forty-nine—wow, okay, first letterbox he looked at. Like what he was about to do was . . . written in the stars.

He rolled his eyes at himself and parked, then scooped his magazine from the passenger seat.

Like most of the houses in town, Cora's had a weatherboard façade with a creaking veranda that Jason hoped didn't harbour any snakes. The veranda was crowded with brightly coloured pots and garden ornaments. Plenty of places for a snake to hide.

He jogged to the front door, searched under the pots. Nothing but bugs and loose soil until he finally found the spare key under a terracotta frog and let himself inside. The hallway was . . . not what he expected. White, white, white and a splash of steel. Minimalist. Industrial—

An alarm blared through the house, rising and falling in rapid beats.

Crap. He retraced his steps to the entrance—
Call Carl.
He called Carl.
"What's the code to the alarm?"
"What?"

He peeked out a window. The noise had the neighbour opposite opening his door and squinting in his direction. Jason spoke louder over the noise, repeating himself.

"What alarm?"

Foreboding uncoiled in his gut. "*Cora's* alarm." He thought of the key under the frog. Not a pot plant, but close enough. Right? "Forty-nine Gum Drive."

"That's right."

"Terracotta frog?"

"Frog? I'm so confused right—oh wait. Fat frog with the twisting tongue?"

"Yes."

"That's the neighbour's. Forty-six."

Earnest Point Police
@earnestpointcops

Maybe it's not always about saying sorry. Maybe it's about not doing it in the first place.

Chapter Fourteen

B rilliant. He'd broken into a stranger's house.
Not exactly what he'd had in mind.

Mumbling *fucks*, he scampered away from the windows through which emerging neighbours might spot him and out the backdoor to a yard of grass, a fence taller than him, and some scruffy lavender beds.

Not much he could do except cry behind a bush until the siren and Neighbourhood Watch—stopped. God. How long did an alarm wail on for?

Twenty minutes?

He dropped his phone and Google's unhelpful search to the grass and palmed his forehead. No, wait. How long had it been so far—

Five. *Five.*

Let him turn to dust right here and be done with it. He couldn't handle any more oopsies. If this were his town, if he knew the neighbours as *Jason*, he'd be able to laugh something like this off. Hell, he'd rock up to them and explain the situation and get them to find him the code. But he wasn't Jason making a mistake. He was Carl, and no one here would expect this from Carl. They'd think he was simply up to no good, and Carl might be known for all his follies and subsequent fines, but that didn't make him a criminal. Jason couldn't make the neighbours uneasy about Carl.

He let out a slow breath to calm himself. At least this oopsie he could get out of without anyone the wiser. If he could just wait out the torturous sound.

The alarm cut out.

Fantastic. Sirens must be on a shorter timer here.

He crawled forward for the phone he'd tossed away a second time—

Boots. A shadow.

That rather impressive belt . . .

Owen. Hands on his hips. Incredulous. "It's been thirty minutes."

"Does it help if I tell you I'm very, very sorry?"

Owen adjusted his casual police cap and stretched out a hand. Jason hauled himself up with it.

"Dare I ask . . .?"

Jason blurted it all out. How he'd intended to break into *Cora's* house, but somehow ended up in the wrong one. Don't all these houses kinda look the same? Oh, he wasn't planning on *stealing* anything. Just wanted to mess about with her stuff. Er, not mess about in a creepy way: drop a few clues around, like parenthood quotes, and a frilly doll. That all sounded nutty. This was all about horoscopes . . . "Anyway, I meant to help, not to harm. I could've sworn this was 49 Gum Drive."

"The Dallas's letterbox lost a screw. The six swung down into a nine."

"See? Not entirely my fault? I might get away with it? How did you turn the alarm off?"

"A quick call to the owners. And you left the door unlocked."

"Bollocks, I also dropped the magazine in my rush outside.

Would you mind hiding the evidence?" Jason winced. "Unless, ah, that could get you fired. Oh, shit, you should probably arrest me and do everything by the book." It was all over. A silly alarm, ruining everything. As much as he wanted this to go away, he wouldn't risk Owen's job over it. Reluctantly, Jason held out his wrists.

Owen took one of them in a steady grasp and dragged him to the back fence.

Jason stared at him. What exactly did he intend? He wasn't expecting resistance, was he? No need to push him against the fence and forcibly restrain him from behind.

"If you want me from behind you can ask, Owen. I'm not running anywhere." Jason willingly turned himself around and locked his arms behind his back. The grass was softer here and his feet sank into the soil, pushing him off balance. He toppled forward into the fence, catching his cheek and shoulder on the wood.

"I'm not sure what you expect to happen here, but either option is wide of the mark." Owen helped him off the fence and turned him around to dark eyes full of uninhibited joy.

"Um, what would be hitting the mark?"

Owen brushed a thumb over Jason's scratched cheek. "Give me the car keys."

Jason fished them out of his pocket. "Did you know it was me immediately?"

"As soon as I spotted my car. I had to tell Jane to let me come in on my own. She spotted it too."

"She's clever."

"She probably isn't far away from figuring it all out, Jason."

Jason didn't . . . hate the thought.

But Carl.

Cora.

Showing her she was loved was supposed to help unlock the secrets. That was . . . why he was here.

"Now, give me a foot."

Jason gulped down his thought, returning his attention to Owen and his shaded smile. "Hm?"

"I'll boost you over the fence. Meet you in ten at the store."

The thing with boosting was . . . it was all kinds of intimate. Especially the way Jason did it, flapping about, grabbing Owen's shoulder and smashing his groin in the face of the law as he tried to recapture the right alignment. Ultimately, all Jason achieved was knocking Owen's cap off his head and wedging himself onto a wooden fence with a few delinquent nails popping up in places.

"Good lord, Jason. What are you doing?"

"Making love to a fence, apparently."

"Enough of that, you'll make me jealous."

They laughed, a flushed face meeting . . . another flushed face, and Jason managed to rip himself free and tumble onto the bank on the other side. The ripping bit turned out to be quite literal.

The back seam of his jeans had split. Quite a bit. Thank God for flannel. He tied the sleeves around his waist and managed a few polite nods on his route back to the convenience store. One look in the shop window—he shrieked and pulled lavender and grass from his wild hair. The chafed cheek looked fabulous too.

He was being hailed from within the store. "Carl, Carl."

It took him a moment to locate Patricia in the bread aisle.

He ducked in and met her and her basket of freshly baked goods. "I thought you were on today," she said. "Always messing it up."

"You're in good hands, either way . . . Mum."

Her keen eye dropped to the flannel around his waist. "New style."

"Yep?"

Why did his heart always hammer like this? Why was it

impossible to think of something to say? "Nice choice of bread."

This just wasn't his day.

"Nice choice of boyfriend," Patricia motioned to the windows, through which Owen could be seen striding toward the store.

"Yes!" Saved by the boyfriend. "I gotta . . ."

He raced out, got caught in the door, lost his flannel to chomping metal, and crashed into Owen. In his peripheral vision, he was very aware of Patricia watching them. He whispered, "Quick! Act like you're in love with me!"

"Act?" A raised brow.

"Patricia's watching us. Actually, if you could grab my arse . . ."

"I'm in uniform, sweetheart. As much as I want to, I can't grope you in public."

"Oh, right, no, of course. Just thought you might help me conceal my *Emperor's New Clothes* boxers, but understood." He pulled himself a decent step back.

"Conceal your *what* boxers?" Owen glanced at the reflection of them in the shop window, and in seconds he had his cap off and was holding it behind Jason. "Into the car, quick."

Owen herded him all the way into the passenger seat and slung himself behind the wheel. "*Emperor's New Clothes* boxers?"

"It sounded better than naked butt?"

A groan. "What are you doing to me?"

"Yeah, sorry."

A flash of smoke in those dark eyes. "*Torture.*"

But surely not as tortuous as the silence between them as they drove back to the station? Jane was waiting for Owen with her arms crossed, leaning against the patrol car.

Behind the wheel, Owen scrubbed his face and looked at him. "I have a surprise for you."

"I'm not in the metaphorical doghouse?"

"Metaphorical or literal"—Jason perked up at Owen's words—"for the time being."

That was . . . "What's the surprise?"

"I wanted you to discover it on your own. But this is the only way I can ensure no other shenanigans take place before my shift ends." Tyranny glinted in his eye as he once more handed over the car keys. "Drive straight home."

"Can I collect Mary first?"

A sigh. "*Then* drive straight home. Do not pass Go. Do not collect $200." He dangled the keys over Jason's open hand, pausing. "You any good with needle and thread?"

"Not really?"

"Happy to hear that." Cool metal pressed against his palm, and Owen opened his door. "Wear my spare jacket around your"—he gestured—"and don't throw those pants away."

Jason found Alex calling Mary into the car.

Jason slid up to them.

Alex jumped, knocked his fingers on the back door, and shook them with a suppressed grunt. "Why is everyone sneaking up on me today?"

"Sorry." Jason petted Mary's head. "Did you two have a special outing planned? Or could I steal her back?"

"Oh, would you?" Alex looked relieved. "Only, I need to patch things up after this morning and Sammy's a little allergic."

Jason crouched to Mary. "You hear that, you're coming back home with me." He glanced at Alex, plucking stray dog hair off his T-shirt. "Will it be difficult, patching things up?"

A sigh. "He was upset about still being a secret. More than I thought."

"Surely he understands your position."

"Yes, he does. He's been very patient too." Alex blushed, looking along the magnolia-lined street toward Owen's car, past it perhaps. "I know he looks big and burly, like he's one of the strongest men in the world, but he still has feelings."

Something stirred uneasily in Jason's stomach; he swallowed to keep it down. "I hope you find a way to make everyone happy."

"If I can't, I'll have to make a choice."

"Choice?"

"Come out and keep them, or . . ."

"Hide from family and be miserable," Jason murmured once Alex had reversed out of the driveway.

Mary pressed close to his side, and Jason resumed petting her. Then grabbed his phone and called Carl.

"Uh-oh," Carl answered with a nervous laugh. "What have I done now?"

"Nothing," Jason said, and paused. "I mean, other than flashing your mum."

Silence. The rustle of leaves in a breeze. The clank of garden equipment next door.

"The reason I'm ringing is . . ." He rolled his shoulders and stroked Mary rather desperately. His words came out in an impassioned burst. "Cora needs to know you love her. That you know she had twins and adopted us out, and you've found your brother, and you still respect her. Hold her dear in your heart."

"I can't—"

"Sooner or later she'll find out. Don't let her turn down living with a good man and his daughters because of an uncomfortable conversation."

A stir of movement came from behind him. He spun around, heart hammering. No, he'd imagined it. Just an empty porch.

"I . . . Don't say anything. Not yet. I will tell her. After the wedding next week. I just need a little longer. Keep up the act, please? It'll be easier once Pete's married."

And easier to be in Wellington, where Jason could wait and see if his blood-relatives ever reached out to him. Carl would tell Cora and Patricia he *knew*, but he would keep this twin-swap to himself. It'd be up to Cora if she had any interest in reaching out to Jason.

Yes. In Wellington it would be easier.

He frowned over the achiness in his chest.

"Mary Puppins," he whispered and hugged her. "I've messed everything up, haven't I?"

Mary did not yip.

To distract himself, he focused on the less stomach-churning moments of the day. Or stomach-churning in a different way. As they drove back home, he gave Mary an account of his day and attempted to describe the depth of his earlier mortification. Mary listened patiently from the passenger side, panting happily as he got to the part about his pants ripping. "There's a part of me that never wants to meet his eye again." Jason sighed and parked the car in the driveway. "But a much bigger part that will not be able to help itself."

He clapped his thigh for Mary to follow, and used the key Owen had given him yesterday. He stared at the blue metal as he kicked off his shoes. There was something about it. How Owen had hesitated as he'd pulled it out of the living room dresser drawer. Jason had been too caught up in other emotions after breakfast; lost in his need for space, he hadn't paid attention. But now . . .

Jason gripped the metal. Had this been the key he'd had cut for Hayden? Was this the key that had once represented his hope for a happily ever after?

Mary nuzzled his hand and Jason carefully slipped the key into his pocket and patted it. He'd make sure nothing happened to it.

He glimpsed his reflection in a mirror, twisted and . . . Oh, wow. That was truly obscene.

He laughed. Really, what else could one do? "Let's find a snack, Mary—"

Quite smartly, he halted in the doorway to the living area. The couch had been shifted, the TV repositioned at the opposite corner, the rug shifted.

And there, all gleaming and pretty, was his surprise.

Earnest Point Police
@earnestpointcops

If you reckon breaking the law is exciting, have you heard of Netflix and chill?

Chapter Fifteen

Mary squeezed past him, fur under Jason's trembling fingers. She sniffed around the room, reorienting herself, and finally stopped at the piano stationed proudly against the wall.

Both feet and heart thumped as he arrowed toward the stool, the open fallboard, and a square card propped on the music rack.

> Got Carl's permission to have this moved here for as long as you need it. Hope this makes you feel more at home,
>   Owen

Oh God, it did.

He patted the stool for Mary to jump up and took a selfie of them grinning in front of the piano. He sent it to Owen with a kissy-smile.

```
Jason: Thank you

Owen: You're welcome
```

Jason: Will you be hungry when you get home? I'd love to make you my favourite pumpkin sage fusilli

Owen: Will eat earlier in the evening, but I'd love to bring some of that in for tomorrow night's dinner

Jason: Consider it Tupperwared

He touched a smooth ivory key and winced. It'd need retuning. What a perfect way to spend the evening while Owen was working—making food for them, tinkering with the piano. He kept his torn jeans on the entire time, part laziness and part anticipation born of Owen's cryptic—or maybe not so cryptic —parting words. He might have, approaching midnight, spent a few naughty minutes in the bathroom with Owen's lubricant, and he definitely might have stripped himself of everything but the jeans and draped himself over the piano afterwards.

Car lights beamed through the front windows and cut out, and Jason shivered, minty breath fogging the polished wood. He'd left a single lamp on in the lounge for ambience, and fried sage spiced the air from earlier. All in all, not a terrible scene to come home to after a—let's admit—rather crazy day.

Owen let himself into the house quietly and, quite like Jason had earlier, came to an abrupt stop in the doorway. His cap was off, along with his shoes and his utility belt, but the rest of him was neatly uniformed.

He laughed softly and moved easily into the room, plucking at his shirt buttons. He dropped his shirt over the back of the couch and strolled perfect musculature towards Jason.

Jason bit down on a grin and aimed for coy. "I've been very, very bad."

A few lazy yips.

"Mary, I'm roleplaying."

More gentle laughter, and Owen sliding behind him, a warm press against his back. A nuzzled kiss into the crook of his neck. "It's almost like you plucked the fantasy from my head."

"A bad boy getting his just desserts?"

Owen inhaled deeply and the suction pebbled goosebumps on his skin. "You, in my house, over a piano."

He groped the hole in his jeans and sank a finger home, and Jason loved the unquestioned nature of it.

Owen's pants dropped to his feet, a *churring* slide down the back of Jason's jeans, and then—blunt, thick heat and a million nerve-endings met as Owen pushed into him.

It felt different this time. Better, dare he say. It wasn't the position, or the satisfying clunking of keys as he'd dropped a hand to the ivory, or even the idea he was being rammed hard against a piano. It wasn't even the naughty thrill of Owen fucking him through a glory hole in his jeans. Or the way Owen didn't unzip him.

It was . . . the fact he hadn't taken off his socks. The way it was all so *relaxed*. Like Owen hadn't been surprised at Jason's offering. Like he'd come home to a boyfriend who had needs and was more than content to gratify them.

It felt like fucking, yes—God, GOD yes!

But it also felt like being taken care of.

The rock-hard thrusts into him were each their own revelation. He'd been curious about sex with a man, and had anticipated far more pain and awkwardness, but this stretching hit all the right nerves. He was soaring, higher and higher toward release.

He whimpered and slunk fingers to his crotch—

"Hands where I can see them, sweetheart," Owen growled in hot syllables at his ear.

Jason smacked his wrists against the top of the piano, and

Owen thrust into him a dozen more times before he peeled open Jason's straining zipper and freed him. Jason gasped at the efficient touches, the ribbed fist stroking around him, faster, faster.

With a bright flash, Jason exploded long and hard against the side of the piano, and Owen was another three groaning pulses behind. Spilling deep inside him.

Jason sagged against the piano, blissed out and boneless. He pouted and shivered when Owen removed himself. To go from having him so close, so *intensely* close to . . .

Owen turned him around and tucked him against his chest. He kissed his forehead. "You didn't have to wait up for me, but that was lovely." He pulled back just enough to read Jason's expression and smiled, satisfied. "Still feeling okay." A rub over his arse cheek.

"I can't seem to get enough." Jason glanced at the piano and laughed. "It'll be easier to clean, but . . ."

"But?" God, the tender way Owen brushed fingers through his hair . . .

"I shouldn't have bothered tuning it."

OVER THE NEXT FEW DAYS, JASON TUNED THE PIANO A COUPLE more times . . . Worth it, of course. Then Owen promised that would be it for a while; time to give the old instrument a break. Jason was fairly hopeful he was talking about the wood instrument. The wood and *ivory* instrument.

While Owen spent his evenings at work, Jason played for Mary—mostly practice for his Erwin Schuloff rehearsals, which were approaching . . . all too soon. He shoved the thought to the recesses of his mind and cooked and Tupperwared to Owen's Spotify playlist—instrumental classics and a lot of Crowded House, and yes, Jason could get behind it.

He even started humming the tunes at work. While ringing up customers, while mopping aisles, while selecting a Catbernet for the not-misogynist who'd come in for more. But the time kept draining away.

When Cora came in one lunchtime, rounded the counter and sat on his chair flipping through a magazine—eyes glazed, like her thoughts were somewhere else entirely—he couldn't help wishing he could be a part of seeing her happy. That he could show Cora she was loved.

The store doors opened, and Alex raced in waving his phone, puffed. "Carl, did you see the tweet?"

"What tweet?" he asked, pulling his phone from his back pocket.

"Earnest Point Police." He laughed. "Owen needs saving." Jason swiped and tapped.

BREAKING NEWS: Sundale School's grade ones take Sergeant Owen Stirling and Jane Marsden hostage. Their demands: three books read aloud and donuts for everyone. @Carl'sConvience Can you save us?

He looked between Cora and Alex, grinning. "Alex? Do you know how to work a till?"

CORA LED THE WAY TO THE GRADE ONES' CLASS AND WAVED AT Craig's youngest girl before adding her box of donuts to the stack Jason was carrying, and dashing off back to work. Kids swarmed the boxes, jumping and crying out in all shades of over-sugared delight, while Jane and Owen talked with the teachers.

Owen had been reading to the class when Jason first came through the door, but when he'd finished the book he'd grinned and, with a devilish wink at Jason, sent the kids scurrying over to him and his donuts.

Jason had never juggled so much enthusiasm before and he was laughing as hard as the rest of them.

He glanced across the room and found Owen in his dress uniform, smiling, arms crossed, hat in his hands. Smart indeed. Crisp and well put together, a man of principle, a man who would put himself at risk to save others. A man who'd done as much for Jason many times. The diligent and ethical service medal he'd been awarded glinted in slants of light coming though the classroom window, his golden hair a halo. Gosh, he shouldn't stare so openly.

Jane weaved her way over to the donut station and nabbed one before they were all devoured. "Thanks for getting us out of a tight spot."

"Thought you weren't supposed to negotiate with terrorists?"

"Negotiate? We caved the moment they made their demands."

Jason laughed, and Jane sent him over to Owen to help carry the bags of show-and-tell gear back to the patrol car.

Owen was still engaged with the teacher; Jason simply mimed, collected the zipped up duffel bags and heaved them over his shoulders. He trucked them over the school quad to the patrol car on display in the middle of the carpark.

"Jason," Owen called.

Jason dropped the bags either side of him and turned around. Owen jogged toward him, hat back on his head, grin underneath it. He slowed his approach to a stride and gestured to the bags. "You didn't have to take them all."

Jason winked at him. "We're boyfriends. Your bags are mine to carry too."

Owen laughed. "Look, Jane offered to do the second half of my shift today."

"Why would she offer that?"

"She overheard my parents on the phone earlier—they went to visit Mum's sister today and they'll be heading back via our place. Jane needs me to cover one of her late shifts next week so it works for her if we swap. What do you reckon?"

"Finally."

Owen's eyebrow twitched.

"Your photo album keeps taunting me. I want stories."

FIVE HOURS LATER, JASON GOT STORIES.

They sat crammed on the couch after spaghetti and home-made meatballs, tartan dress and tartan pants on either side of Jason. Mary panting at his feet. Owen behind the couch looking over their shoulders, one hand lazily playing with the back of Jason's hair.

"And that's Owen on his third birthday."

Jason grinned at the boy with his eyes rolled back, shirt off, covered in chocolate. "Drunk on his cake, I see."

"Oh honey, that's not cake."

Owen groaned and fingers squeezed his nape when Jason couldn't stop laughing.

"This one was just before we discovered a tiger snake in the backyard. Look, you can see it in the background . . . there."

"Jesus."

"He was the bravest of all of us," Nathan said, with a proud glance at his son. "Always brave, my boy."

"You should have seen how competently he handled *my* snake."

Fingers stilled in his hair. Renee and Nathan blinked. Then Mum quickly jerked a finger toward Owen in a school bag. "Oh, and *this* one . . ."

Jason had never been so thoroughly spoiled. He couldn't

even pick a favourite photo, although the cringey teenage ones were something. The soccer uniform, hands on hips, and a mouth full of braces was fun. So was his first date picture, his mum hugging him dressed in rainbow tartan. He liked the glimpse of roses. Old-school romantic.

"All I need now is to see you in sexy leopard print leotards," Jason said once the parents were gone and they'd finished the after dinner clean-up.

Owen swiped suds off Jason's nose with a small, secretive smile. "I saw Mum gave you one of my resume photos."

"It's in my wallet right where a boyfriend pic belongs." Jason pecked his lips and moved to the piano. "I've been practicing something for you."

Owen strolled up to the window beside the piano and clasped his hands behind his back. While he stared out through the darkened night to Carl's property, Jason let his fingers dance out the rendition of "Don't Dream It's Over" he'd been working on.

When he finished, Owen was quiet. His shoulders lifted on a large intake of air and slowly fell.

"Was that not . . . what you're into?" Jason murmured.

"No, it's . . ." Owen turned and sat next to Jason on the stool. His arm blazed with heat. Something more intense filled his gaze. "I didn't think I could let myself again."

The soft way he spoke, the frustrated edge to it, followed by the soft chuckle. "But here we are."

Owen glanced at the instrument Jason had spent so many hours tuning over the last few days.

Oh, *oh*. So what? He didn't care. He pressed back against Owen's arm. "It's okay. Over the piano works for me."

"Jason . . ." The groan had Jason looking at closed eyes.

"What? We can."

A long breath. "Not tonight."

"Sure? I really don't—"

"Why did you play that song?"

"You have a few Crowded House playlists on your Spotify account. I thought you'd like it?"

"I do. Especially that one. Especially you playing it."

"I like how it's an Australian band but there are Kiwis in it. Sort of like, look how great the two combine. Can I play you another one?"

"'Fall At Your Feet'?"

Jason kissed him and began, their lips still sliding together. To his surprise, when he pulled out of the kiss Owen started singing. It almost made him stumble. The soft deep quality of it. The careful timing. The changing of all the hers to hims.

A nervous thrill wove through his veins. This was something . . . magical. The energy of their music thrummed through him, too much to process—he was achy everywhere, inside and out. He abandoned the last few notes. "Owen?"

"Yes?"

"Please . . . please?"

"C'mere."

THE MOMENT OWEN SANK INTO HIM THAT EVENING—ONE long, deep push—was ferociously fulfilling. Jason's breath had hitched at how intimate and intensely trusting the moment was. Each thrust pushed him closer and closer to the cusp of . . . a much-needed release. And it delivered on one aspect, but not the other. Not the one trapped on the tip his tongue.

Not the one trapped behind that thought in the back of his mind: the days were ticking down. Soon Carl would return and all this would be reduced to memories.

Unless . . .

It burst suddenly off his tongue the next morning, at breakfast. "Maybe you can visit? After the wedding?"

Owen's head snapped up, his hand still pouring their coffees.

Jason leaped across the kitchen and tilted the carafe upright before caffeinated goodness overflowed from the mug.

"Visit you?" He didn't sound keen. Maybe Jason had gone a step too far, thinking this was anything more than a fake-boyfriend gig with an expiry date.

"You don't want to know what my life looks like in Wellington?"

"No."

So . . . emphatic.

Jason grappled for a grin but it felt weak, waning by the millisecond. "Are you coming to the stag night after work?"

"Jason—"

Jason's phone rang. Pete. For the fifth time that morning. He'd become more and more nervous as the days went by and had called Jason increasingly for his thoughts, his input, his assurance the replacement band wouldn't pull out at the last minute.

Jason took the calls with amusement and sometimes—when snuggly with Owen—reluctance. Right now, he took it with relief.

"Pete!" He left Owen and Mary and found a patch of sun out on the front porch. Warmth over the lingering shiver.

"I know, I know. I just want to make sure you're okay being designated driver."

"Oh no, fine. I absolutely don't care for drinking and all the distraction that comes with it."

"At least you'll have an advantage with Angus."

Did he *want* an advantage with this Angus? "Uh, right. Yeah."

When Pete rushed to his next call, Jason stood in his sunshine, acutely aware of Owen and Mary moving around in the house. He thought he heard the creak of a floorboard close to the door, and hurriedly dialled Carl.

Who . . . who was entertaining someone in the background. He sounded a little out of breath. "Jason here."

Definitely entertaining, and playing Jason while he was at it. But this wasn't the time to ask. "Just wondering . . ."

"Wondering?"

"Exactly who is Angus? . . ."

The answer had him pressing the phone against his throbbing forehead.

Another floorboard. Owen or Mary or both were close.

Stomach hoppy, Jason fiddled with his phone, working the appearance he was concentrating hard. Not to be interrupted. His fingers slipped to his Grindr app and then he was scrolling through those messages with Daniel, before Jason knew.

Call Me Carl: That's the gist of it all

Daniel: I could swing that. If you're absolutely sure it's only a few weeks. That this would be fake.

Call Me Carl: Kinky promise

Call Me Carl: Pinky Promise!

Call Me Carl: Probably should warn you I get myself into unintentional trouble sometimes

Daniel: No worries. I know how to navigate trouble

Thinking back on it, that might've been a clue. Owen was a cop after all, dealing with trouble was his actual job. The rest of the thread went into specifics about the when and where of their date, all to the point and frank.

If you're absolutely sure it's only a few weeks. That this would be fake.

Jesus. There it was, clear as crystal.

A low rumble and a warm shadow. "Why are you sniffing?"

"I'm not." He sniffed again.

"Sweetheart."

Jason shoved his phone into his pocket and scratched his finger on the house key he'd slipped into these clean, tear-free pants earlier. His finger came out bleeding, and Owen curled an arm around his shoulders and steered him into the kitchen. He was careful as he wrapped a plaster around the torn nail.

The thing was, Owen had drawn the lines and it wasn't his fault if Jason had stomped all over them, made them barely recognisable. The lines were still there.

In a week this fake boyfriend act would be over.

He had a choice: get all sniffy about it, or—

He curled a determined hand around Owen's nape and crushed him against his lips.

"Jason," Owen murmured. "I think we should talk."

Jason stiffened and shook his head. "I don't want to talk. I want to . . ." He dropped to his knees and looked up. "Please?"

Desire flashed in Owen's eyes and he shut them with a hard swallow. "Do you know how hard it's been for me to resist you in this position?" A hand pushed through Jason's hair; nails skidded lightly over his skin, scattering goosebumps. Those dark eyes on him again. "On your knees in front of me."

Jason butted his head against Owen's hand, wanting more.

"You're not playing fair, Jason."

"I'm not the Libra, Sergeant Owen Stirling. Sir."

Owen hissed in a breath, really gripping Jason's hair now, like he was desperate to give in. There was a tremor vibrating through him, and Jason leaned in and nuzzled his head against powerful thighs. "Let me start here?"

"Start?"

"I'd finish you off here, too, except . . ."

Owen stroked his hair back.

Jason flashed him a pre-emptively sympathetic grin. "I might need you still hard to help me with something?"

Fingers paused. "What?"

Jason slid his fingers up Owen's jeans. He popped open a button, and then worked the zipper. "I'm in a little pickle? Speaking of pickles."

Owen laughed. "I'd prefer if I wasn't compared to a pickle."

"Oh no." Jason pulled all of him out, so hard, so heavy. "You're a right cucumber."

"*Jason.*" Hearty laughter—

Cut short by Jason flicking his tongue against that glistening head.

"You're impossible."

Jason lapped more of the saltiness from him and then sucked him into his mouth with a moan. He looked up innocently. Well, as innocently as one could while gorging on cock.

It was a good thing the kitchen island was behind Owen, because with the next inch Jason took, his knees buckled. "God. I will talk with you, though."

Jason came off reluctantly. "Not now."

"After."

"I have to help set up the party. Then there's the party."

"Tomorrow, then."

Jason took more of Owen into his mouth, right until he hit the back of his throat.

Owen gasped. "We'll go to the beach. We'll talk."

Sand, sea, stray wallabies along the shoreline. The candid picture of Owen's family, laughing. Owen's special spot.

Was that where he broke up with all his lovers and fake boyfriends?

He made a garbled sound, and it wasn't from choking on Owen's mounting eagerness.

"God your mouth is amazing. Oh, Christ. I'm way too close."

Jason clamped his hands on Owen's thighs, steadying him as he drew off, lips swollen and delightfully salty. "Not yet, please?"

A cocked eyebrow above dark sparkles in his eye.

"I need to practice something before I meet Angus tonight."

"Angus?" he said sharply.

Jason didn't mind the sudden glare he was receiving. It made his belly hop. He squeezed Owen at his base, feeling the pulse under his skin and the silkiness surrounding all that primal potential. His voice got husky. "Could you try bucking like a bull while I ride you?"

Earnest Point Police
@earnestpointcops

Glad you're all having fun out there. Just a reminder, we'd appreciate not being invited to any parties.

Chapter Sixteen

In the middle of a padded, fenced area sat a massive steel-welded bull, covered in fake fur, with a model horned head. As well as Jason had clung onto Owen's bucking frame, there was no question: he'd be no match for Angus.

Eyes like the devil bored into him, a challenge that Jason was very happy not to accept.

The bar heaved with energy. Drinks had been circulating the Stag Crew for the last hour, music pulsed, and cheers rang through the space every time someone got bucked off Angus.

Pete had not yet relaxed, and when he finished taking yet another call, Jason swiped his phone. "It's your night to go wild."

Pete laughed and shoved a stressed hand through his nicely waxed ginger quiff. "That was about our rehearsal dinner. Our booking's been cancelled due to a fire. Now instead of doing it the night before the wedding, we'll have to hold it at Trinity tomorrow."

Jason hailed the bartender for a beer—Pete's earlier pick—and slid it over.

"Thanks, man." He took a large gulp. "Never get married.

I mean, do, but . . . last minute weddings are a pain in the arse. Not the fun kind."

"Tomorrow isn't so bad. It gives you more time to concentrate on the big day. Plus no nasty hangovers."

"Silver linings, Carl. That's why you're my best man." Pete looked at him, grin dropping to something softer. Serious. "It wasn't . . . we weren't . . . but I love you as a friend."

A beautiful sentiment, but he wasn't sure he'd want Carl to have heard it.

Pete bumped his shoulder. "Your boyfriend's here. Jesus, I still can't get over that. Gimme my phone. I'll make the rounds. Oh, and Carl?"

"Yeah?"

Waggling brows. "Show Angus what you've got."

A wan smile. "I'm sure you'll all be very surprised."

Laughter tickled his nape, and Jason sank back against a firm chest and arms that immediately steadied him at his hips. "You're here."

Owen kissed him under the ear, eliciting a delightful shiver. He smelled like he'd come straight from a shower, lavender and bergamot. Crisp, damp hair combed over his cheek.

Pete paused in his retreat to gape and shake his head, and Jason happily added to the show, spinning around to capture Owen's mouth.

"Good evening so far?"

Jason murmured, "Just got better." He ushered Owen to a booth that had just freed up, but instead of slinging himself opposite, he slid onto the same bench and pressed their thighs together, craving contact. He wanted to make the most of every minute before the damn beach and their 'talk' tomorrow.

"Are you growling?" Owen was watching him, amused.

Jason fiddled with the empty metal napkin stand. "Yes. Uh, because of the serious lack of napkins. Pete paid good money to hire this place. It's making me grumpy."

"You want napkins?"

Jason looked at him. "I want . . . napkins."

Leaning towards him, "You could always ask for them."

Ask.

Jason's breath hitched. His heart started making a ruckus.

He swallowed, but it didn't settle. He stood abruptly, so hard he banged his thigh and pain lanced through his leg. Even so, it was the triple-quavers in his chest that held his attention.

Owen raised a brow, but his silent *What's going on?* was cut off by a gruff yell.

"Christ, Carl!" A stocky man with an alpha grin lumbered over, the air around him thick with interest. "Blake. Remember me?" An undeniable slinking glance down Jason's length followed. "Last year of high school?" Another lingering look. "You've changed."

"I'm a completely different person."

"Niiiice. You know mate, you and me should really catch up. Grab you a drink?"

Jason had no idea who this Blake guy was. An old friend? Crush? Boyfriend? Frenemy? He opted for a safe smile-and-nod.

Owen shifted on his bench, eyes rooted on Blake, arms folded squarely against a puffed chest. Jason motioned towards him. "Blake, have you met Owen? My boyfriend."

Blake's expression cooled. He eyed Owen up and down, and shrugged after a moment, life flooding back to his smile. "Yeah, okay. Let's get this party started. Beers?"

Owen cleared his throat and spoke. He didn't sound like himself at all. Rather blunt. Like he might still be on the clock. "Carl and I are the designated drivers tonight. If he decides to drink, fine, but *I* will be driving him home."

Jason swung his head to Owen.

Owen smiled stiffly, and Jason looked from his fake boyfriend to Carl's high-school someone. Sergeant Owen Stirling seemed particularly cold with the man. Like he knew him. A petty criminal he'd dealt with before? Or was he a bully to Carl, and Owen knew? Or was this . . .

He sank back to the bench, knees weak. A silly smile crept onto his face.

Blake swung a last look between them, shrugged, and pissed off to the other end of the bar.

"I thought you wanted napkins?"

Jason propped himself on his elbows and sighed dreamily. "I need to *ask*."

A flash of colour dropping onto the opposite bench stole their attention.

Hayden, with a wobbling smile. "Kaden couldn't make it tonight. I don't know anyone apart from the grooms, and they're far too busy on that bull. Hope you don't mind?"

Jason kept a light smile on his face. Grabbed the napkin stand and started squeezing. "I *live* with Owen. I suppose I can share him for a few minutes."

Incredulously, "You're living together? What's that like?"

How utterly tactless.

Not a single shadow on Owen's face gave him away, but Jason had felt the roll of the bench cushion as he'd stiffened.

Owen's house key seemed to vibrate in Jason's pocket, like it was hauling in air to scream. Or maybe that was just him.

As calmly as he could, he said, "I am protected, provided for, and appreciated. I've never felt more at home."

A warm hand curved over his thigh, and Jason was "The Marriage of Figaro", Mozart. He fucking *fluttered*.

Hayden flushed. "I . . . of course Owen would be great to live with. Sorry if I sounded sceptical, it was . . ." He laughed, throwing up his arms in defeat. "I'm jealous. I gave up a good thing and I've been trying to convince myself I've found something better, but the truth is . . ." He swallowed and glanced across the bar. "Kaden isn't here tonight because we're not together anymore. Apparently I'm self-centred and shallow, and in fact, he's very right."

The first time Jason had met Hayden, he'd hated him for showing off his new and better man. For being thoughtless and rude.

Now, Jason sensed Hayden's insecurities. Now he *felt* the deep sincerity in his admission.

Now, he hated him more.

Owen's hand came off Jason with a squeeze and he patted the back of Hayden's hand sympathetically.

Hayden blinked rapidly, tears glimmering in his eyes. Apologies at his lips. "Sorry, Owen. This isn't appropriate. I shouldn't have said anything. I should never have left you. I shouldn't have said that, either. I'm messing this up. I've messed everything up."

"Hayden. Deep breath." Owen glanced at Jason. "Would you mind getting some water? And asking for some of those napkins?"

Turned out, Jason was a truly awful person. He got water and napkins, but he also got himself a double shot of vodka and downed it before returning.

Owen thanked him, but after a flashing smile, he turned his attention back to Hayden.

Each one of Hayden's sobs and apologies wrenched through Jason, killing every flutter that had ever leaped to life inside him.

The finale of Tchaikovsky's 6th symphony. Steeped in despair. Loneliness. He might just sag under the table and curl around Owen's legs, crying into the hems of his pants.

He murmured to Owen to take his time, headed back to the bar, and ordered another shot.

At least Owen had promised to drive him home if he decided to drink. Pete wouldn't be too thrilled, but Owen could drive them all back. He would, too. He was that decent. Thoughtful. Kind . . .

Hayden wanted a second chance.

Oh fuck. Owen's horoscope had predicted this. *For single Libras, old lovers will return and new passions may be reignited.*

Fiery vodka burned his throat.

Light and fun sexy times are highly likely.

Another two shots, please.

Dark browns and reds blurred when he glanced towards the mechanical bull. Instead he saw blond. He saw Owen under him, trying to keep a straight face as Jason rode him, one arm lassoing over his head.

And then it wasn't him on Owen, but *Hayden.* "Fuck off."

"All right, mate." It was Blake at the bar beside him, raising his hands. "Just grabbing a drink."

Jason startled. "Sorry, not you. I was talking to . . ." Well, the truth wouldn't do. "To Angus."

"You want Angus to fuck off?"

"*Buck* off . . . buck that guy off."

"You usually a bad sport?"

Jason was having a crisis here! Drink had hit his system and the room had a slight tilt, but it was nothing to the topsy-turviness in his chest. "I just . . . I would take care . . . I would hold on forever."

Blake hollered to the operator across the room that they had a contender, and a few moments later Pete's mates were chanting his name, and a few moments after that . . . Jason was being pushed toward a massive steel beast. "Go on, then. Prove it."

Oh. Um. Asterisks! Side note! Huge disclaimer!

Fingers kept prodding his back. Pete was whooping for him, too.

Owen! Save me!

But Owen was saving Hayden. Who'd *hurt* him.

What if he hurt him again?

Jason clenched his fists, and then he swung himself on the back of that bull. Prove it? He'd prove that he would hold on. That he'd take all the care in the world.

He grabbed the strap, gripped tightly with his thighs, lifted his head to glimpse Owen across the room. Where was he?

He had to find him. The machine shifted under him and then lurched. No, he couldn't come off now. Goddammit, he was trying to be symbolic.

He jostled through six seconds of mechanical bullying—

Smack!

He hit the padding with all the grace of a discombobulated duck.

Groaning, he pushed up on shaky arms. All the orchestra in tears. *He couldn't hold on.* A sign of its own?

Hobbling out of the arena, he met Pete shaking his head. The whole room spun, drink and disappointment deteriorating the last of his sense.

"Mate, you are off your game."

"Guess my arse is too sore from other things." He shoved out of his flannel shirt. "And this stupid thing kept flapping. In the way."

Pete found his overreaction amusing. "Yeah, yeah. Blame it on the flannel. By the way, while you were flirting with Blake—"

"I was *not* flirting."

"Chill. I know. You guys were just chatting, I was exaggerating." Pete eyed him oddly. "Anyway, Owen asked me to tell you he's going home with Hayden. Apparently you'll understand."

Going home with Hayden.

He'd understand.

Hayden *was* the man Owen had fallen in love with at first sight, and Hayden wanted Sergeant Owen Stirling Sir back, and Owen and Jason were only fake-dating anyway, so Owen's choice was inevitable.

He nodded and nodded and slunk away to the booth where his heart had beat out two very different melodies.

The napkin holder was full of napkins, but they were the wrong napkins.

He tipped his head against the back of the booth and closed his eyes. He must have fallen asleep, because Owen's deep voice murmured close to his ear. "You don't look great, sweetheart. Let's get you home."

Jason sighed. Home sounded good. But if he were going to dream about Owen, couldn't he say he looked fantastic?

Heat at his shoulder.

Jason startled, his eyes pinging open. Not dreaming!

A chuckle. "No, you're not."

Owen hovered over him in sexy jeans, polished shoes, and a jacket over a button up. Look at that face. Chiselled, strong, clean-shaven. Blond hair gleaming like a halo. A body that knew all the ways to turn Jason on. So unfair.

To have this wondrous revelation, and not be able to keep the contents of it.

"What did you say?" Owen asked, helping him to his feet.

"You were jealous of Blake."

"Yes."

"You like me."

A pause. "I do."

But did he enough? Was it fair to want more than *like* when they'd only known one another two weeks?

And was it possible for Owen to fall in love at first sight *again*? When he'd proclaimed so adamantly that he wouldn't? When Hayden had admitted his feelings?

God, it was unreasonable of Jason to be so upset about that. Owen and Hayden had so much more history . . .

It was just . . . he liked Owen very, very much.

Jason swallowed a groan. At least, he thought he swallowed it. Didn't liking Owen mean he wanted what was best for him? What made him happy?

"No matter how tough people seem"—Jason felt up Owen's generous biceps, and then gazed deeply into dark, possibly bewildered, orbs—"they can still hurt." A swallow. "Your very smart nephew told me that. Made me think of you and my stomach dropped like a bad album."

Owen led him through a cheering crowd and out into the cool, dark night. Fresh air hit his face. Owen slung his jacket around Jason's shivering shoulders and pulled the lapels. Jason looked at him. "Am I making sense?"

A smile. "Are you worried about me, Jason?"

"He broke you before. I-I don't want it happening again." Jason shoved an arm into each sleeve and headed across the parking lot to Owen's car. Owen caught and steadied him at a misstep. Jason paused and rubbed his forehead. "I understand that first horoscope of yours now. About fearing history repeating itself."

"If I recall, that horoscope suggested Libra be brave and *not* fear history repeating itself. And Jason," a finger lifted his chin. "I don't fear it. Especially not after tonight."

Because . . . of him?

Or because Hayden had shown himself truly remorseful?

He couldn't ask. His smile ached. "As long as you're happy."

"I will be."

Owen opened the door for him and Jason crumpled inside. The drive back home was quiet, Jason leaning his head against a vibrating window. The pricklish heat of Owen side-eying him every other minute made him fear the loss more. What if soon he wouldn't have it?

What if tomorrow Owen let him know he was returning to Hayden? He groaned when Owen led him into the house. "Do we have to go to the beach? Do we have to talk?"

"What's that, Jason?" Owen said, helping him out of the jacket, his shoes.

He leaned against the wall so the hallway would stop swimming. "Just . . . please don't invite me to the wedding."

"Wedding?"

"You know, if you and Hayden tie the knot."

Owen stared and stared at him, and then Jason's world tipped upside and he was head-butting Owen's back. A smart smack met his arse, and a few steps later, he was deposited on Owen's bed. "That's my limit of you for tonight."

 **Earnest Point Police**
@earnestpointcops

Just a friendly reminder that losing your keys is not a reason to call 000

Chapter Seventeen

Well done, Jason. Things were really under control now. Crapity crap. How did he get into this mess? They were supposed to be fake boyfriends with a clear end date, but Jason had gone ahead and lost himself in the act until it didn't feel like an act at all. The ache when he thought they'd have to create a break-up scene . . . It was enough that he'd lost all rhythm when Owen had so fervently rejected the idea of seeing him in Wellington. The only good in it was how it'd . . . it'd put things into sharp perspective.

A bitter-sweet realisation; it'd been beautiful and hopeless in a single breath, until . . .

Until Owen had puffed out his chest and got all wonderfully 'mine' in front of Blake. Owen had at least *some* feelings. Whether he knew them . . . whether he *wanted* them . . . But it meant there was a chance, right?

Or there had been until Hayden showed up.

Hayden.

Scowl, scowl, scowl.

Were there not enough obstacles to overcome? Telling his brother that he'd fallen for his sort-of-nemesis, breaking it to the town that Jason had been fooling them, bracing for Cora and Patricia's reaction—and possible rejection. Not to mention that tiny wee issue of, oh, telling Owen what he was feeling.

Could he convince Owen to give *him* a real chance over Hayden?

And before any of that, could he maybe, just maybe, delay Owen taking him to his beach spot to potentially break up with him?

"Enough frowning into space, Jason." Owen picked himself up off the adjacent armchair where he'd been showering Mary with cuddles. "Let's go for a drive."

To the beach? Jason gulped and scampered behind him. "Only if I drive!"

Owen tossed him the keys and they slipped into the car. Jason opened his mouth and closed it, then leaned forward for a kiss but his heart rammed too much in his throat, so he veered to the glovebox instead. He pulled out one of the chocolate bars Owen stashed in there and ripped into it like he hadn't eaten breakfast an hour ago.

Owen clamped a palm on his thigh and Jason jumped.

No one was watching, Owen didn't really have to do that. But he did do it. He always had, with or without an audience. Hope and fear were a nauseating mix in Jason's stomach.

Owen seemed to be profiling him. "I think there's something we want to talk about."

"No, no! Who needs talking?" Jason started the car. "Comfortable silence is all the rage, you know."

"Jason—"

Jason pressed a finger to his lips. "Shhh. There you go."

After a good five minutes sharing in this 'comfortable silence' while Jason drove as far inland as possible, Owen folded. "You're acting all out of sorts."

Out of sorts. Yes, *that* would most definitely delay the departure speech. "Actually, now you mention it, I am feeling . . ."—Jason looked at him—"sick."

"Sick?"

"Very sick."

Owen directed him to the nearest safe place to pull over and as soon as the engine cut out, he had his belt off and was clamping a hand onto his forehead. "No fever. What are your symptoms?"

"Oh, you know . . ."—unrequited feelings of passion—"headaches. I don't seem to have an appetite." He eyed the chocolate wrapper in the console. So did Owen. "Much of one, though I'm trying to keep up my sugar intake. You know, to help combat the body's stress."

Owen's gaze raked carefully over his face, assessing, a slight gleam in his eye. "Is that right?"

"I just can't concentrate on anything else."

"Else?"

Crap. "The pain."

Owen's lips quirked. He hesitated and glanced out the window. "I know what it is."

"You do?" Not squeaked at all. "You do?"

A hesitation. "I have to say, I'm glad to hear this isn't a sickness you're overly familiar with."

Jason caught his eyes. "I have never felt this sick in my life."

Another pause, a nod, and then a cheeky dimple appeared as he refocused on the road. "Must be one hell of a hangover."

Hangover.

For a moment there he'd thought the cop hadn't fallen for it.

"Fresh air's the best remedy," Owen said. "Swap seats, I'll drive us to the beach."

"No!"

Amusement. "No?"

"I just mean . . . salty places never help when I'm sick? Yes. I should avoid them at all costs."

With a humming sound, Owen said drily, "Then salty *places* will be off-limits."

Jason did a double take. Did that . . . did he mean . . . Jason blinked at Owen's lap.

"*All* salty places, sweetheart." A wry grin. "Until you're feeling better about visiting them again."

He knew Jason didn't want to go to the beach.

He'd been playing him.

And now he was saying no more fun until they'd had their talk finalising their finality?

Outrageous.

Jason got out of the car and stomped past Owen to the passenger side. "This sickness will take a very long time to recover from."

The plea for Owen to reconsider for his own sake was met with nothing more than a quirked lip.

Fine. No more sex with Owen. Didn't matter. He loved *all* the things he did with Owen, and he'd enjoy those to their fullest, without stupid conversations redrawing the lines between them.

"What do you want to do, then?" Owen murmured.

"I want to hang out with your friends and family. Alex, Hannah, Jane, your parents. So long as there's a crowd." And no way for them to 'break up' until he'd figured out how best to get Owen to give him a *real* chance.

Owen side-eyed him. "You *sure* you don't want us to go to the beach?"

A desperate nod. "Let's, ah . . . let's . . . deliver donuts to the guys at the station!"

"Nothing I love more than heading to work on my day off."

"You can stay in the car. I'll crack a window." Jason flashed him a wink. "Just look at us functioning."

It'd been the first thing he could think of, this little trip to the station, but Jason was going through with it. He picked up donuts and everything.

Owen didn't come inside. Not because he didn't *want* to, but he'd been snagged into conversation with a local and had whispered for Jason to save himself. By the looks of it, Owen would be stuck out there for a while.

A relief, really. A few moments without all that glorious distraction would give Jason the space he needed to figure out his plan. Mary accompanied him inside, where he was ushered through to Jane and co. Jane was on a break and had settled herself onto one of the chairs in the corner of the room—the same one Jason had sat on when he'd first come there. She had a paper open to the daily crossword on her lap and was pencilling in a word.

"Hello? I come bearing donuts?" He flipped the lid. Jane set down her paper and gave the box of donuts a mighty welcome.

"What brought this on? In trouble again?"

Jason slumped onto the opposite chair and petted Mary behind the ears. "You could say that."

She raised an interrogative brow, and Jason . . . Jason told her everything. Not only because she could be quite intimidating when she put on her cop face, but also . . . with her the stakes were at their lowest. He liked her, he really did, but her rejection would not pain him as much as others' would.

Also, he felt she ought to know sooner. So that . . . so Owen could have someone *he* could talk to about everything. He needed that support.

"Please, it was all my doing. Owen warned me it wasn't a bright idea and I ignored the advice, and then he helped me because he's amazingly good-hearted and kind. And I, of course, go and screw everything up. And then . . ."

Somewhere at the start of his detailed summary, she'd started an *Oh Crikey* mantra, interspersed with comments like, *I knew something was off. Got on much better with you. Didn't make sense.* And later, *Oh, you absolute fool. So that's how the alarm went off!* And lastly, *Some trouble indeedy.*

"What do I do?"

His stomach was twisting so hard by the end of his explanation that his voice came out breathless.

Jane covered her eyes with the crook of her shirt, and when she dropped her arm, she was in cool control.

"Owen deserves to be happy . . . Jason."

He sank his chin to his chest. She was right, but it . . . his heart . . .

She leaned forward and looked at him sternly. "*Hayden* would not be my first choice for that."

Jason snapped his head up.

Mary's ears pricked and she trotted away from them toward the doors, and *Owen.* Yikes, Owen! Jason flustered like he were about to be caught in some illicit act, and on instinct he thrust himself into the nearby closet.

Through the door, he heard Jane laughing and pictured her, quite rightly, shaking her head. "What on earth are you doing?"

Fair question. He sagged against a shelf of paper. "Could you distract him for five minutes while I figure it all out? Then set me loose?"

She left him with sage advice. "Don't hide longer than you have to."

Her footsteps retreated, and he let out a long breath. The last time he'd been in this closet he'd been tucked against Owen, admitting the truth about who he really was. Now he was here again, fretting how to tell him even deeper truths.

He would just have to . . . ask. And hope.

Oh, God. Would that be enough? Didn't he need some kind of romantic gesture?

His phone shrilled loudly in the quiet space and he fumbled in his urgency to deal with the sound. His finger swiped, answering the call. Not exactly his intention, but—"Carl? Just a quick call. We're moving toasts to before the main course. Mum thought it would be better."

Toasts?

"You'll be up first."

Toasts?

He shut his eyes and swallowed a groan. He whispered "That's perfect" into the phone and hung up.

What on earth could he—

He straightened. Maybe this could . . . be his gesture to Owen? It could be a toast to Pete and Nick on the surface, but the *subtext* . . . if he were clever, Owen would know he was really talking to him. All without giving himself away to the wedding party! Yes. A win-win by all accounts, and then after his toast, Owen would . . .

Either sweep him into his arms.

Or march him directly to Break-up Beach.

Light flooded into the closet. "Thanks, Jane—"

Not Jane. That large frame could only belong to Mr July. Jason lounged nonchalantly against the shelves. "Fancy seeing you here."

An impressively arched brow.

He patted a shelf beside him. "Took a moment to reminisce."

Wow, Owen could really hold an expression.

"Would you like to reminisce with me?"

"Beach. Now."

Jason's heart jumped into his throat; he stormed past and

out of the closet. "Can't! I just learned I have a toast to write and practice for the rehearsal dinner."

"I'll help you, and *then*—"

"And then I'll have to help Pete. Yes, he'll need me to make sure everyone gets to the right restaurant and on time. Oh, damn, that puts a dent in our day off together. I guess I'll have to make it up to you tomorrow." He charged ahead, past Jane shaking her head, and out into the foyer. "I'll head to the store."

A vexed laugh.

"Meet you tonight!" Jason didn't look back.

~

HE DID, IN FACT, HAVE TO GO HOME AND CHANGE BEFORE dinner. Alex wasn't supposed to be working the shift, but when he'd learned Jason and Owen would be there, he'd called in to see if they needed any extra help. Someone had just called in sick, and so Alex drove Jason past Owen's for his suit—Owen absent—and they headed to Trinity together.

"You're sure about working tonight?"

Alex nodded. He seemed . . . a little out of spirits? "You and uncle Owen will be there so it'll be better than other nights. And paid, so."

Jason side-eyed him. "Anything else going on, Alex?"

Alex banged his head against the back of his seat. "I just left Mum a note. Saying . . . everything. And that I can crash elsewhere after work tonight, if . . ."

"You can always stay with us."

"She'll be reading it when she comes home. Any minute now."

"Nerve wrecking."

A nod. "I messaged Gramps and Grandma, too. Because

I'm crazy apparently. But also, I just can't have it on my chest anymore?"

"Did you tell Owen that you'd tell them? He'd want to be there for you."

"I told him. He . . . said I was doing the courageous thing and he wished others could be so brave—be honest, no matter the consequences. He said he just wants to settle down for real. Sounded kind of sad, actually."

Jason stared down at the cue-cards he clutched. "He said that? He sounded *sad* saying that?"

Alex parked in the staff carpark, facing the sun as it sank slowly toward dusk. "I mean, you have to really know him to hear that. But . . . I do. He was gently sad."

Oh God.

Gently sad. The subtext was about him, wasn't it? He . . . he had these feelings about Jason hiding his identity? He wanted Jason to do the courageous thing?

Owen wanted to settle down for *real*. He was tired of faking. He wanted . . .

"He said something about checking up on Hayden later, needing to clarify where he stood with his boyfriend. Has he spoken to you?"

He wanted to clarify where he stood.

To be with Hayden, Owen had to separate from 'Carl'. But Jason had rebuffed every attempt to break up with him. Owen needed Jason to reveal himself or, at the very least, contrive a very public break-up where Jason was the bad guy.

Heat prickled behind his eyes and his stomach churned. He slouched through shafts of peach light toward the restaurant's side entrance.

At the awning, his phone rang and Jason gestured pathetically for Alex go on without him.

A rather throaty voice rumbled down the line. Carl. "Ah, Jase. Guess you're about to head to the rehearsal dinner?"

He sure kept close tabs on everything happening with Pete. "Yes."

"Look, I know this is . . . would you . . . keep me on the phone during the toasts? Secretly? I . . . I just want . . ."

"To torture yourself?"

"To be there. From a distance."

Jason felt Carl's pain. Having to let go of something beautiful. Having to do what hurt for the happiness of another.

Jason didn't like Hayden. He didn't *know* Hayden.

But Jason's opinion didn't matter. Owen had said as much when Jason had been afraid of meeting his parents. No one's opinion mattered but Owen's own.

Could he just go ahead and drown in a puddle of misery?

"Ah, there you are," Pete smacked his back. "Just came out for a breath of fresh air and not at all for a sneaky ciggie. Starters will be out soon." A waggled brow. "Looking forward to your toast."

Jason gave a wan smile and carefully slipped the phone inside his inner jacket pocket, right over his aching heart. Carl could probably hear it cracking.

Pete lit his cigarette and sucked in deeply. "Thanks for making sure Darla got here. She's already cracking everyone up inside. Y'know, you should chat. She knows everything about star signs and stuff. She'll be able to tell you what crazy things will happen to Capricorn this month."

"*Capricorn*. I mean, right. Yes."

Smoke curled out the sides of Pete's mouth. "Speak of the devil."

A sprightly older woman with a glitter in her eye emerged from the side door and stole the cigarette from Pete. Instead of stomping it out, she took a drag herself. "Who're you calling devil, young man?"

"You?"

"Brazen, Aquarius."

Pete grinned broadly. "Carl, meet my great—great? —aunt."

"Just one great will do." She smirked and looked Jason up and down shrewdly. "This the boy whose heart you crushed?"

"Darla!"

She coughed out smoke and decided that was the moment to squish it under her foot. "Rather thoughtless of you to ask him to be your best man."

"He was happy to do it!"

"He wants you happy, of course he said that."

Pete looked sharply at Jason. "No, he's fine about it. He's been just fine. You're fine, right?"

Jason stiffened; he could feel the weight of the phone against his chest, the equally saddened Carl listening in.

Carl had flown to New Zealand and asked his twin to trade places with him to avoid the hurt of watching the man he still had feelings for marry someone else. 'Carl' had gotten a fake boyfriend and still Carl continued the ruse. No, he was not fine. But Jason . . . understood. "I want you happy."

Darla's phone burst to life and she struggled to answer an incoming video call. "Pete, help me, dear."

Pete helped her and then Darla was calling out delightedly. "Becky, Zane, how are my lovebirds?"

"As lovey as always!" one said in a chipper voice.

The other, more restrained, "Checking to see you got there all right?"

"Oh, fine. Very good flight. The stop in Melbourne was wonderful."

"We look forward to meeting you in Wellington after the wedding!"

Wellington after the wedding.

Jason shivered.

Would he be there too?

Darla shuffled between the potted plants edging the sunset-soaked parking lot, and Jason looked over to find Pete frowning at him.

Quickly, he copped his way inside.

What a mess he'd gotten himself into! If he could just get through this night and start sorting it out tomorrow.

Twenty-odd wedding guests had arrived and were seated around a long table at the far side of the restaurant. Jason rounded the dozen other tables glittering with candles and flute glasses, and—

He crashed into Cora.

"What are you doing here?"

She blinked at him. "I'm here with Craig. It's our second year anniversary."

Jason gestured to Pete beside him to discover he'd continued to his guests. "I'm here for Pete's rehearsal dinner." He looked Cora up and down. She wore a short mint green dress with matching shoes and bangles. Her hair was swept up and delicate earrings gave off a green sparkle. "You look pretty." He saw her glance at her table and Craig, who was smiling nervously, patting his jacket pocket. Checking he'd brought the ring, perhaps? God, now he looked, he caught the agitation in Cora's fingers, the way she kept swallowing, the shifting of weight from foot to foot. "You having a good time?"

She nodded and bit her lip on a smile. "Yes. But I . . ." She gazed at him. "Actually, I'm glad to see you here, Carl. It has to be a sign."

A good sign, he hoped. Perhaps he ought to say something to cinch the goodness of this 'sign'? *What?*

"Well, I better"—she gestured to her purse—"freshen up."

She moved toward the ladies' and his chance was gone. Maybe later in the evening.

Jason's spot at the table was at the end, closest to the stage and the grand piano. The tables were different, they'd been rearranged, but he was sitting exactly where he'd been sitting with Owen on their first date. Uh, fake date.

He scoured the table, again. Definitely no Owen.

Alex was assigned their table, and they shared a grin as he took Jason's drinks order. "Uncle not here yet?"

"Maybe he took Mary out for a walk and lost track of time?"

Or maybe he'd decided enough with faking. He wasn't going to come. He'd rather hang with Hayden.

When Alex came back with drinks, and then starters, Owen still hadn't shown up. Briefly, he'd hung up on Carl to fire Owen a quick message, but no reply. Carl was the only one glued to Jason's line.

"Holy shit," Alex murmured and almost dropped a plate of oysters. Jason followed Alex's surprised gaze across the restaurant to three figures piling in at the door, being led to a round table near the window. Hannah, and Alex's tartan-loving grandparents.

Jason pressed a napkin to his mouth. "Did you know they'd be here?"

Alex quietly hyperventilated next to him. "What do they want? Is this . . . an intervention?"

"Maybe they're here to offer support. To tell you they're here for you."

Alex shook as he pretended to be busy refolding a napkin. "Oh my God. Jason. Make them go away. Please. What if . . . what if . . . I can't right now. I have to work. I can't cry. I—"

His breathing worsened. Sounded uncannily like Patricia had after he'd fed her pineapple. He patted Alex's back. God, he felt those *what ifs* . . . the anticipation, the fear of rejection. The impending *loneliness*.

"Deep breath, Alex. It's okay. I promise, it'll be okay."

"How do you know that? How can you be sure?"

How *could* he know that? How could he be sure when he kept finding excuses not to say his truths?

Pete's parents dinged their champagne glasses, the signal for toasts to begin. Him. He was first. His chair rumbled over the floor as he stood and fumbled for his cue cards. His heart banged against his phone. He felt Carl's doing the same. A moment of twin solidarity.

"Pete and Nick—"

"Speak up," someone called.

Another, "Use the microphone on the piano." Addressing the restaurant, "You won't mind five minutes of toasts from the stage, will you? Rubbish, Peter, you're just sour because I beat you at bowls this morning."

A chorus of laughter and glass-tinkering started, and Jason was ushered to the platform. Alex scuttled along with him and handed over the microphone.

Immediately, Hannah spotted her son and made towards him.

Tartan watched, riveted.

Cora looked up from her own intense candlelit moment.

Pete kissed his fiancé's fingers, interlocked in his own, and smiled towards Jason.

Gripping the microphone, Jason cleared his throat. He'd been on stage a thousand times before, in packed theatres, but this small-town audience . . .

"Pete and Nick," he began again, shaky voice magnified, filling the room. "You're—"

Owen entered the restaurant with a purposeful stride and effortless grace.

"*Beautiful.*"

 **Earnest Point Police**
@earnestpointcops

The only lights we want blinking right now are your mid-winter fairy lights.

Chapter Eighteen

The fabric of Owen's crisp suit shimmered under ambient light, moulding to all his hard contours. His gaze moved around the room, calm, controlled, until it landed on Jason. Electricity surged through him and his harsh breathing crackled through the speakers.

Owen stepped out the way of waitstaff and paused, folding his arms. Dark eyes fixed on him with all their knee-buckling intensity. Something lurked in that gaze. Something heavier than all the times Jason had looked at him before.

Gently sad.

His grip tripled on the microphone. Another tap on glass had him turning his head to Pete and Nick, acutely aware of Owen watching, waiting.

The words on his cue cards hovered at the tip of his tongue. *When you met, you knew. This is the real thing. This is what I've been waiting for my whole life and you bravely jumped in with both feet. You knew when you find the person who makes you happy, you want to have that happiness for the rest of your life. And you want that life to start right away.*

Another glance at Owen. A shift in his posture. A spark in his eyes that shot tingles right through to Jason's feet.

What if . . . *what if* . . .

His heart jammed into his throat.

Carl.

Cora.

Rejection.

Loneliness.

Owen.

Hannah had crossed the room, only the width of a table from Alex. Alex dropped a flute glass. It shattered, causing heads to turn.

"S-sorry," Alex stammered.

"Honey, please. Talk to me," Hannah said quietly.

More heads turned. Owen ripped his gaze from Jason and started for his sister, but the town cop getting involved only drew more attention.

Jason heard Alex's squeak. The squeak of the dying. A prayer for release from this mortifying realm.

Owen had always said sooner or later there'd be a fallout. He'd promised that someone would get hurt, and he was right.

There was no way out of this mess without causing pain.

The only choice he had was the decision, Carl and Cora's hurt? Or Owen and Alex's? The family he'd originally come for, or the one he'd been forging since?

He could lose everything, of course. He could lose all of them in the space of seconds, Owen only stopping to thank him before racing off to propose to Hayden.

But.

He felt loved enough . . . and more. *He* loved enough.

He dropped himself onto the piano stool and slipped the microphone into its holder.

∼

Rebecca Clarke's "Piano Trio". The piece Owen had first heard him play.

Difficult. Intense, stormy, passionate. A piece ingrained into his fingers since he was seventeen. A piece that elicited urgency, *allegro agitato*. A piece that felt like the pounding of his heart.

But . . . this wasn't just about *his* heart. There was only one person here he needed to prove anything to, and for him . . .

Without another second of hesitation, Jason shared his secret.

The notes ripped through him with the fear. He finished a short section with a flourish and a flush. *What next?*

Silence.

Shock and confusion.

His pulse ticked up a notch. Owen, where was Owen—

"The fuck." Pete. Stunned. Bright red.

A choking sound. Devastation. "Oh God. *Jason.*"

Cora.

He swung his head to her. She stood there in mint, under dim lights in the middle of the room, tears tracking mascara down her face.

She sobbed, turned and ran, worried partner on her heels.

Renee and Nathan watched Cora leave, grimacing.

The phone at his chest buzzed and buzzed. Frantic messages from Carl. Who'd heard everything. Knew the gig was up.

Another strangled voice. Quieter. Alex. "What's going on?"

A heavy clearing of a throat, and Jason's pulse echoed Chopin as he snapped his gaze finally to Owen.

To Owen and his warm eyes, the steady set of his jaw. Owen beheld him like he . . . like he was proud. Thankful. Relieved. Jason didn't know quite how that would translate, but it was enough.

"I can explain," Owen said.

Jason jumped to his feet, voice echoing in the microphone. "It's my mess to clean up." He gazed around at half the towns-folk he'd gotten to know, the faces that were feeling like friends; neighbours; *family*.

All the faces he'd deceived.

"I'm sorry." The words fell as a whisper, but they carried. "I'm not Carl. We just swapped lives for a while." He looked imploringly towards Pete.

Pete shook his head over and over. "But you're . . . I can't believe . . ."

"We're twins. We didn't find out until a few years ago."

"Twins. And he . . . he didn't want to be here anymore? How long?"

"A few weeks. Until the wedding. It hurt him too much to be your best man."

"Knew it," Darla exclaimed across the table. A dozen eyebrows snapped upwards in her direction and she rubbed her hands together. "Carry on."

Pete blinked rapidly. "He never said."

"He wants you happy. He's"—Jason pulled out his phone —"he's been here the whole time. He just couldn't be *here*."

A harsher voice. Alex. "What else have you lied about? Have you been leading my uncle on?"

"Alex," Owen said tightly.

"No, Owen. It's not okay. You were happy, I could see it, and he's tricked you."

"He's done no such thing."

"You—you knew?"

Jason's fingers grazed cool ivory. "I asked him not to tell anyone. I asked him to pretend with me."

"Pretend. So you're not . . . boyfriends?"

Jason swallowed hard. Shook his head. "It's all fake."

Alex flushed, furious.

Jason had counted on a lot of hurt, but he hadn't been ready for the power of Alex's. Alex pushed past his stunned mother and followed in Cora's footsteps, running out the door.

"Owen, please explain." Hannah's voice was quickly drowned out by a chorus of other people asking questions and the slap of Jason's shoes.

He raced out the door, leaving Owen with half of his baggage while he raced after the other half.

Fresh air hit him with a salty tang and he spied both Cora and Alex in the distance, one splitting to the left at the beach, the other, the right. Jason didn't hesitate. He worried for them both, but one was even more his family than the other. He needed to express that.

He caught up with Alex at the sea's edge. Sun on its last rays at the horizon. Waves lapping gently at the shore. Sand sinking under his feet.

The beach Owen went to with his mum, dad, sister. Alex and Mary. The beach Jason had been avoiding all day.

The beach that had finally caught up with him.

Alex dropped onto a wrought iron bench at the stone wall, and Jason perched next to him. They stared at the darkening water.

"I kept a lot of secrets."

Alex shut his eyes.

"I lied about a lot of things. My name, where I work, who my friends and family are. But, Alex? I didn't lie about any of my feelings."

"You faked being in love with Uncle Owen."

Jason's heart pounded. "Did I?"

Alex's eyes pinged open.

Jason continued, "I came here curious about who the other half of my family were. I didn't realise I would make another one I don't want to lose."

Alex blinked and threw his arms around Jason, holding him tight. "I'm a hypocrite. How could I get so mad when I kept my secret from Mum for much longer? I should've understood. I was frightened of their response, so frightened, and you distracted Mum. You gave up your secret to help me manage the fallout of mine. I should've just hugged you. I'm sorry."

"Don't be. I mean, if you hadn't run out, I'd still be sitting there fielding a town full of questions." He paused, wincing. "Which I left your uncle to do. Damn, he really is always saving me."

"I'm sure he likes it. I'm sure he wishes he could do it forever."

Jason laughed, rolling his eyes. "I'm sure."

"I'm sure." A soft feminine voice from the shadows.

Jason jumped, and Cora came into view beside him, dabbing her eyes with a tissue.

"Cora?"

"I've been walking up and down here to calm down. I heard everything."

Jason stared at her, the lump in his throat refusing to budge even a little. "You were curious about where you came from." She sniffed and dabbed her eyes again.

Alex pressed his palms to the bench. "I should go—"

"No. I don't want there to be any more secrets." She let out a deep breath, and laughed. "Horoscope promised this would be quite the month of family changes. Wasn't wrong."

"Cora, I'm sorry. I just . . ."

"I snuck into all your shows when you played in Melbourne and Sydney. You wanted to know where we all ended up. If we're all . . . happy."

"You watched my performances?" He gestured for a tissue and Cora, sniffing, fumbled for a fresh one and handed it over.

"You're remarkable. Both of you are. My Jason. There hasn't been a day where I haven't thought of you."

Jason's tissue was already damp.

"You'd never have had the opportunities you did if . . . It hurts, but I'm still convinced it was the right thing. For both of you. I was too young, too immature. I ran away from home and never told anyone I was pregnant. My parents weren't exactly the type who cared, either, you know? I only had an aunt who cared. Patricia. You were born on her bathroom floor, where I had been hiding out those last months while she was overseas. I lived like a hermit, and drove forty minutes every other week for groceries and to a doctor so no one saw me. I was good at hiding it. She got back as I started having contractions, and she was so shocked. I pleaded with her to not tell anyone. She agreed to help. Took us to the city to adopt you both out. Only Patricia, she got attached. She wanted you both, but she didn't have the money or the time for two, so in the end . . . well, you know the end. We came back here and she pretended she'd been the one who had the surprise baby, overseas."

A shuddering breath. From all of them. Alex clasping Jason's hand for support.

"We've all kept secrets. They felt right at the time. But . . . this weight off my chest, it's . . . freeing."

"Yes." Jason paused. "Cora?"

She met his eyes.

"Just because you weren't ready to be a mum then, doesn't mean you won't make a good one now."

"W-what?"

"You know what I'm talking about. If he asks, say yes. I hope that's enough sign for you."

"What if Carl . . ."

"Carl knows. He loves you, too."

"Too?"

"Yes, too."

She nodded and nodded, and swiped more tears, and laughed. "Look at us! We could be a television drama. With a happily ever after."

"Wouldn't that be nice."

"I'm sure of it. Sagittarius and Libra make a great match." She gestured behind him, and Jason turned.

There, not more than six feet away in the last glimmer of sunset, Owen sat, palms planted on the stone, listening, observing.

He stumbled in the sand, tripped, and scurried up again. So smooth.

Smirking, Owen slipped off the wall and moved over tussock and sand towards him. Jason wanted to bolt, but still he was unsure in which direction, and before that—

He held out his finger—*just a sec*—and chased after Cora. "Wait." She paused, eyes just like his hitting him in a way he wasn't sure he'd ever get used to.

He held up his hand.

Tentatively, she lifted hers. Warm palms, and one by one, pressed fingers.

With that ghostly touch, she left. And it was just Jason and Owen, and Alex legging it over the wall, leaving them alone.

Breezes whipped and whistled.

Jason thrummed erratically, every goddamn inch of him. A lightbulb that didn't know if it would turn on, or go out for good.

"Hayden?" he called out, a question.

"There is no Hayden," Owen called back.

Jason bolted—

Right into Owen's spreading arms. Owen caught him around the hip, the thigh, stumbling back in the sand.

Laughter curled around them as he transported them to the bench. He kept Jason astride his lap, warm thighs under his arse, hands rubbing up and down his arms to ward off any chill. If such a thing could possibly exist right now!

That blond head shook, lips twitching. "You sure don't do anything by halves."

"Is that a crime, Sergeant Owen Stirling, Sir?"

A devilish glint in dark eyes. "The jury's still out on that one."

"I'm sure you could get me off . . . scot-free."

Owen turned his head toward the navy sky and laughed. Jason curled against his chest, forehead against his neck, and whispered, "There's really no you and Hayden?"

A long stroke from Jason's nape to the small of his back. "I made sure to clarify that earlier."

"That's why you were late this evening."

"I'm sorry. I needed to be clear with him. He was too drunk last night, or I would have done it then."

"Oh God. Last night!" Jason thought about it. "This morning!" What a fool he was. "I thought you wanted to take me to the beach to break up with me."

"My favourite spot? Why would I taint it with bad memories?"

"You know, that makes a lot of sense." Jason laughed at himself. "I wasn't thinking straight." Another chuckle. "Guess I haven't been this whole time."

"Hmm."

Jason pulled back and looked at Owen. Not an ounce of sadness lingered. Had he . . . had he worried this might not happen? Had he thought Jason might head back to Wellington anyway?

Of course. And Jason had stupidly—oh-so-stupidly—asked him to *visit*. The punch that must have delivered when Owen thought they . . . had something. Because they *did* have something. Didn't they?

Jason cupped Owen's jaw. "Are we really together then?"

"We have been from the start, Jason."

"Fake boyfriends."

Owen clasped his neck and pulled him into a fierce kiss. "There was nothing fake about it."

Earnest Point Police
@earnestpointcops

Copping a feel is a quick way for me to get my cuffs out.

Chapter Nineteen

A powerful quiet settled between them as Jason opened the door. His hand shook as he twisted the key. Clammy fingers made the metal slippery and he dropped it onto the welcome mat.

"Fantastic symbolism."

He rushed to pick it up, burning, and Owen crouched too, scooping it up first. Eyes met his, soft and sincere. Owen peeled open Jason's fist and gently settled the warmed key on his palm. "How's this for symbolism?" He closed Jason's fingers over it. "Yours."

Jason tightened his hold until metal dug into flesh. He swallowed, whispered, "Why am I so nervous right now?"

"It's our first time."

"Uh, we've come home plenty of times."

Owen stood and pulled Jason up and down the hall to the bedroom. He brushed a smiling kiss over his lips. Warm, soft, fleeting. "Not like this. Not knowing it's the start of a future together."

A steadying grasp on his shoulder as they removed their

socks. Suit jackets. Button-up shirts. Pants and belts. Sweeping hands over shoulders, hips. The press of kisses in between.

Owen moved to his drawer. He pulled out lube and the, ah—

He pinched out the cuffs Jason had snuck in there, brow arching. "Fluffy."

"These hands are my life."

Owen murmured, "Mine too."

Jason took the cuffs from him, fingering the soft, malleable form. He wanted to use these, to play around. But . . .

He dropped them back into the drawer.

Owen's eyes glittered, waiting.

Jason swallowed. "Tonight's not about curiosity."

Owen dipped his head and locked their lips together for a long, slow kiss.

They slid onto the neatly made bed, sheets cool under exposed skin, and turned on their sides. He reached out and pressed a palm against Owen's firm chest, soft hairs under his palms sparking heat and shivers, a line of goosebumps pebbling up his arm.

Owen's voice rumbled over their shared pillow. "You want to know what really gave you away, Jason? Other than musical recognition."

"You're finally going to tell me the second thing?"

"The *biggest* thing."

Those beautiful eyes, the humour there, the intense understanding. That mouth curling up at the edges.

A ticklish finger stroked down one side of his face. "*That's* what gave you away."

Jason snapped his eyes up. "Hm?"

"Carl never looked at me like that. It's frighteningly wonderful."

Jason looped an arm behind Owen and closed the foot separating them. "Frighteningly?"

Owen rolled onto him, a blissful, protective weight. "You have no idea how hard it was, watching you figure out you liked me."

Jason drowned in those dark eyes, and whispered, "I don't just *like* you, Owen."

∿

HE HAD A BOYFRIEND. HE HAD A BOYFRIEND WHO HE MADE laugh. Usually unintentionally, but still! No matter how many times they slept together, he just couldn't get enough. They clicked on every level, and Jason spent the next two days glowing.

He traipsed up and down the convenience store, every reflective surface throwing back his smile. He had everything he wanted. A partner to come home to. Someone who found his ridiculous oopsies amusing. Someone who loved him back.

They hadn't said the words aloud, but they quivered between them regardless.

The store doors opened, bringing in a gust of autumn wind and Patricia. He'd been expecting her, but he understood that she might need to take her time.

There was a brief, awkward moment where they stared at one another, and then Jason squared his shoulders and moved to her. "I have a confession."

"I know your confession."

"I have another confession."

Her face softened, amused.

He twiddled his thumbs. "It wasn't Owen who fed you the pineapple." He flushed hard. "I'm sorry."

"For forgetting I'm allergic?"

"For everything."

Patricia hauled him into a hug. "My darling boy, what you

must have been going through." She kissed his cheek. "You planning on staying a while?"

"Longer."

She smiled. "Good. You and I, we're going to be friends."

Jason squeezed her back. He'd never imagined he'd have a family in his life again and here he was, in a small Australian town with two.

Over her shoulder, a new figure strolled into the store. A figure so much like his own . . .

Patricia turned. "Carl. I have a bone to pick with you."

Carl halted, blinking them in, and looked away with a grimace. "Not sure there are any left after Pete."

"You silly, silly boy. You should have just told him it was too soon."

"He knows now. Um, is this a bad time, Jase?"

There was something in the way he said it that had Jason holding his breath. "What's going on?"

"I need, ah. When I've settled everything here, I need to go back to Wellington. Just, um, for a bit."

"As you or . . ."

"I might've gotten myself in a little bit of a situation?"

"Oh, God. We really are twins."

"I promise I'll fix it, I just need more time."

Jason shook his head in disbelief. The pair of them! He sighed. "Don't keep your secret too long, Carl."

"Is that a yes?"

"As long as you do me a favour."

"What's that?"

"Organise shipping for my grand piano."

"Shipping?"

"Your one just doesn't cut it."

Carl blinked.

"I'm moving in with Owen." While Carl gaped, Jason

added, "My job is far more flexible. And we both have family here."

His brother blinked again, and then, "Does that mean you're putting your place up for rent?"

~

THIS WAS NOT FAIR.

Jason scrambled out of the dog house to face Owen's dad. "I was just cleaning it!"

"Without a cloth?"

"It's still in there?"

"Wearing a collar?"

"Ha! This? Not a collar, it's a . . . a . . . choker. Everyone wears them in Wellington."

Eyebrows pinged. "What unique fashion."

"We're the capital of coffee and fashion." He nodded as seriously as he could and pushed himself to his feet with as much dignity as one could muster in a dog collar.

He'd been expecting Owen, since it was past closing and he'd just been on the phone with him. Emerging from the dog house was supposed to be a wee joke. Actually, it was supposed to make up for seeing the photo his mum had brought in earlier. Tween Owen in leotards, gosh. He'd had such a laugh, but he felt a little guilty that Owen hadn't exactly approved the gift. This way, they could both be embarrassed, and . . .

It had nothing to do with the way Owen had plucked at the buckle, the way his fingers moved under the strap, the way the leather came off his neck like a caress . . .

Definitely nothing to do with that.

Gosh . . . thin air in here today.

"I won't stay long," Nathan said, eyes crinkling with humour. "I'm here to invite you to dinner tomorrow night."

Jason nodded. "Yes, we'll be there. Will Hannah come too? We could practice what we'll play at Pete's wedding."

"He still wants you at his wedding?"

"His fiancé insists after, um——"

"Your shockingly brilliant performance at the restaurant?"

"I'll be saying sorry in sonatas for a long time. Do I . . . need to for you?"

A scoff. "No need to apologise, Jason. I already knew. I often head to Hannah's to help in the garden. I was there the day you spoke to Carl on the phone. It . . . made sense. There was something different about you. Owen never looked at his neighbour the way he looked at you. I couldn't understand the change, until I did."

"You didn't say anything."

"I'm a firm believer of people doing things on their own terms." A glance to Jason's collar. "Whatever those terms may be."

"I will never look you in the eye again."

Nathan laughed, and headed out the doors. "Welcome to the family, Jason."

"Sergeant Owen Stirling, Sir," Jason said in a single hurried breath down the phone. "I need you."

"Need me?" Owen sounded far too chuffed.

Jason stared at the open deliveries door and the uninvited kangaroo-wallaby-marsupial standing there surveying just how convenient Carl's store might be.

"I mean, I need urgent help with my backdoor."

Silence.

The kangaroo thumped its tail. "Please come quick," he rang out breathily.

"Jumping in the car now. You're on speaker."

Jason gulped. "What should I do while I wait? Feed it?"

"I . . . don't think you should do that in the store."

"Right. It'll get greedy." Jason scanned the store. Water bottles. "I—I'll wet it."

"Again, something we shouldn't do at the store."

"Outside?"

"That would be an offence."

Animal cruelty, right. Yes. Of course. He didn't want to *hurt* it, just . . . make it shoo. A dozen inches over the threshold and he could just shut the door. "I have to make this go away. A couple of bounces is all it would take."

"You've worked yourself up into quite the state."

"I'm kinda shaking here."

"Hold on, sweetheart. I'll take care of you."

Brakes screeched outside, and in rushed Owen on a gale. Jason glanced to him and back to the contemplative kangaroo, still obscured from Owen's line of sight. Owen moved toward him in long, calm strides.

"You're still dressed."

"Undressing would have helped?" Did nudity assert dominance in the kangaroo world or something? Or maybe he meant waving his shirt around to scare it. Why hadn't he thought of that?

He yanked off his flannel—flannel he absolutely hadn't taken a liking to wearing, and only put on out of habit . . .

Oh my God. It worked. The wallaby-kangaroo bounced out of the store. "Shut the doors!" He sprang forward and yanked it shut, turning around, flushed from the adrenalin.

Owen rubbed his jaw. "As much as I'm surprisingly turned on, Jason, I have to insist we explore any kinks at home."

Jason shot him a confused look.

"Don't look so pouty, pup. We'll play soon, promise."

Pup—oh *oh*. His hands flew up to his collar and he flushed.

Owen moved toward him with a soft grin. "Are you embarrassed?"

"You've got this all wrong?"

"Have I?"

"There was a kangaroo. It freaked me out."

"A kangaroo," Owen said drily, shaking his head.

"Yeah. It was right here."

Owen smirked. "Sure the wildlife won't get too much for you here?"

Jason bit his lip and gazed down Owen's length. "But don't you know? Turns out I'm a fan of snakes after all—"

A small smack came to his butt, steering him towards the door. "I want to play too, Jason. But I'm going to have to insist. *I* choose your collar."

Owen nibbled the back of his neck and tugged on the leather with his teeth. Oh. *Oh.*

That . . . the collar bit sounded . . . He dropped to his knees, panting. "Take me home."

THE END

About the author

A bit about me: I'm a big, BIG fan of slow-burn romances. I love to read and write stories with characters who slowly fall in love.

Some of my favorite tropes to read and write are: Enemies to Lovers, Friends to Lovers, Clueless Guys, Bisexual, Pansexual, Demisexual, Oblivious MCs, Everyone (Else) Can See It, Slow Burn, Love Has No Boundaries.

I write a variety of stories, Contemporary MM Romances with a good dollop of angst, Contemporary lighthearted MM Romances, and even a splash of fantasy.
My books have been translated into German, Italian, French, Spanish, and Thai.

Contact: http://www.anytasunday.com/about-anyta/
Sign up for Anyta's newsletter and receive a free e-book:
http://www.anytasunday.com/newsletter-free-e-book/

Join my Facebook group to chat all things Slow Burn Romance:
https://www.facebook.com/groups/SlowBurnSundays/

You can also find me here:
www.anytasunday.com
anytasunday@gmail.com

Lightning Source UK Ltd.
Milton Keynes UK
UKHW011824120722
405744UK00004B/1099